One Night with Him

by

K.S. Smith

One Night with Him
by K.S. Smith

This is a work of fiction. Names, places, characters, and events are fictitious in every regard. Any similarities to actual events and persons, living or dead, are purely coincidental. Any trademarks, service marks, product names, or named features are assumed to be the property of their respective owners, and are used only for reference. There is no implied endorsement if any of these terms are used. Except for review purposes, the reproduction of this book in whole or part, electronically or mechanically, constitutes a copyright violation.

ACKNOWLEDGEMENTS

To Jo, you are my life, my love. No matter how many book boyfriends I bring to life through my writing, none of them will ever compare to you and the love you have continued to give me these past ten years. Thank you for being you.

To my family – I hope you don't read this and think I'm a complete freak, besides y'all were there for the many "talks" with mom, so blame it on her.

My partner in crime, the person I began this journey with, I cannot begin to express the amount of fun I have had traveling down this road with you. You are my Addison, with a Rose personality. I love you and cannot wait to see where this amazing road leads us, together, always.

Ty – you were my first real five star and I cannot thank you enough. I love that you love this book as much as me and I thank you from the bottom of my heart for your continued support.

And lastly, to the one and only Rachel Van Dyken, your infinite wisdom and loving heart has been a blessing. You have helped so much through this entire process and there are no words that could possibly describe my gratitude. Now get back to Nixon!

Chapter One

The toxic smell of Patron hit my nose and I instantly knew this was going to be a night I wouldn't remember. "Shot! Shot! Shot!" The sound of fifteen women rang in my ears, as I grabbed the penis shaped shot glass off of the table and pressed it to my lips. Tilting my head back I cringed when the tequila slammed into the back of my throat. It reminded me of liquid lava. I could feel the burn all the way into the pit of my stomach.

"You *are* so lucky you're my best friend, because you're the only person I would do a shot of tequila for," I yelled across the VIP section of the club to my best friend.

Addison was spinning herself around the stripper pole, a hot pink boa laced around her shoulders, grinning from ear to ear. It was the weekend before her wedding and we were all out celebrating her bachelorette party. "I knew you'd cave, you can't say no to your best friend, can you?" The words rolled off her tongue in a slur, since she was already six shots ahead of me.

"You're the only person I can't say no to, and you know that!" I smiled as I raised another shot to my mouth. I knew as maid of honor I had some catching up to do. I couldn't let my best friend drink herself into oblivion all by herself, especially not on her last weekend as a single woman. The perks of being Addison Cartwright's best friend usually meant that you had whatever you wanted at your fingertips. In tonight's case, it was the entire VIP section of the hottest night club in town, The Limelight, owned and operated by none other than Mr. Theodore Cartwright, Addison's father. Addison came from money and her family only obtained more of it once her father took an interest in the night club scene. It had benefited us tremendously in college and tonight was no different. Our entire section was raised two floors above the rest of the club and everyone was envious. Bouncers lined all the entrances and only those escorted by Addison herself were allowed in and out, with the exception of me, of course. I was like a second daughter to the Cartwright's, so I had just as much clout as Addison did when it came to the night club.

"I think we need more Patron," I shouted across the table to girls, "and some guys, we really need some entertainment up here, I'm not doing all of these shots to entertain myself." I stood up and scanned the VIP section for one of our servers, but they were nowhere to be seen; so I took it upon myself to make my way down to the second floor of the club to order a few more bottles of Patron and see if I could find any guys who looked worthwhile.

"Excuse me, Hank," I tapped the huge bouncer on the shoulder, "I'm going down to the second floor to get more Patron, I'll be back in a few minutes."

"Do you need a bouncer to go with you?"

"No." I touched his arm to thank him, "I'll be fine, Addison is the one who draws in all of the attention; I can usually go unnoticed." Hank smirked and nodded his head, as I walked past him and down the stairs.

The bar was packed, music blaring; people were pressed together as tight as sardines. I could hardly get through the crowd and up to the bar. I should have listened to Hank and grabbed a bouncer, just so they could have cleared a path. After what seemed like hours of pressing through people's sweaty bodies, I was finally belly up to the bar. I waved to Chris, the bartender, and he was in front of me within seconds.

"What can I get you, beautiful?"

"Four bottles of Patron Gran Burdeos, please." Chris went into the back room and came out with four bottles. "You want me to send them up to the VIP area, so you don't have to carry them?"

"That would be amazing. Can you grab me a water, while you're at it?" Chris gave me a wink and was back in seconds with a bottle of water. "You're the best." I smiled and left a generous tip on the bar for our favorite bartender. I knew if I intended on drinking more tequila, I needed some water to keep me from wanting to die the next morning. So I leaned against the bar and pounded back my water.

"I'm impressed" a deep husky voice whispered into my ear. I glanced to my left and leaning against the bar next to me was what had to have been a model plucked straight out of a GQ magazine.

"Pardon me?" I asked looking him up and down.

"Impressive, I've been standing at this bar for over twenty minutes and I haven't even been acknowledged by the bartender, then out of nowhere you run up here with your tight little ass and smile that would bring a grown man to his knees and instantly you have four bottles of Patron and water within seconds."

I smiled, batting my eyelashes. "I guess those are the perks of having a tight ass". *Did I really just say that?* It wasn't like me to be so quick on my feet, but I was proud of myself. As I whipped around to walk away, GQ grabbed my arm and pulled me back towards him, so I was pressed right up against his chest. Damn, he smelled good, I'm not sure what cologne he was wearing, but it had my senses running on overdrive.

"Is there something I can help you with?" I glared up at this beautiful stranger, who was much too close to my face.

"A drink for starters, I figured I'd have better luck with the bartender if you were calling his name." I turned around in his arms and waved for Chris one more time as GQ nuzzled my neck and whispered into my ear, "and your number would be nice, too."

Chris was in front of me before I'd even put my hand down. I pressed my ass against GQ's crotch as I leaned over the bar and yelled, "Would you get this guy a drink, he's been waiting a while."

"Sure, what can I get'cha, man?"

"A Yuengling, please". Chris grabbed a Yuengling and was back in front of us in just enough time for me to scribble my telephone number on a napkin.

"Thanks, Chris, be sure to put those four Patron's on his tab for the hassle." I grabbed the Yuengling, set it on top of the napkin that had my telephone number scribbled on it, handed it to GQ as he stood there with a shocked look on his face, then turned around and walked away as fast as my feet would move.

There was a reason I didn't drink tequila, anymore, and that was it right there. It made me crazy, example number one, I'd just put four bottles of $500 tequila on a total strangers tab. I hoped he had a great job, because there was no way Chris was going to let him leave without paying for that liquor. I smirked, proud of my quick wit, as I looked over my shoulder just in time to see GQ take a drag off of his beer, his eyes raking over my entire body. My stomach flipped; who in the hell was this man and why was my entire body tingling at the thought of him watching me?

Chapter Two

"Where in the hell have you been? You're my maid of honor, you just can't go disappearing like that!" Addison was standing on top of the table, taking a drink straight out of one of the bottles.

"I'm sorry," I screamed over the blaring music, "I got side tracked downstairs. I promise, no more disappearing!" *Unless GQ finds me, then it's a whole different story.* "For the rest of the night, it's me, you, that bottle of tequila and all of our girls."

Addison grabbed my hand and pulled me up onto the table with her, lifted her bottle as high above her head as she could get it without toppling over and screamed, "You're damn right it is!" All of the girls with us began cheering and the cheering lead to dancing, the type of dancing you do when no one is looking. Oh yeah, between the shots and our screaming sorority sisters, there was no possible way I was going to make it to tomorrow without putting myself into a tequila-induced-coma.

After several hours of dancing on table tops and flirting with the few guys Addison allowed into the VIP section, it was time to call it a night. Addison, along with several of our other girlfriends were on the verge of being passed out drunk on the couches that wrapped around the room. All the while I was making sure everyone who was capable of still standing on their own two feet were getting their things together in order to make it back to the party bus. "Hank, would you have some of the guys help Addison and the other girls to the bus, I think it's time we get back to the hotel." Hank nodded and began to get a few guys together. After several attempts of corralling fifteen drunk women down two flights of stairs and through a sea of people, we finally made it back to the hotel in one piece.

I'd booked us a penthouse suite at one of Tampa's most luxurious resorts, The Bellevue, so we all had plenty of space to spread out. But I'm not going to lie, when everyone got to the room they'd passed out everywhere but the bedrooms and it pretty much resembled the morning after scene of The Hangover. Bodies were scattered throughout the entire suite. I'd finally gotten Addison changed and into bed. Just as my head hit the pillow my phone started beeping. *You've got to be kidding me*, I thought as I stumbled around the dark room searching for my cell phone. Not recognizing the number I reached for the power button to turn it off and ignore the incoming text, but something in my gut told me to open it and see who in the world was crazy enough to bother me at this hour of the night.

WHAT ARE THE ODDS YOUR PARTY BUS IS PARKED OUTSIDE OF MY HOTEL?

WHO IS THIS?
I'LL GIVE YOU ONE GUESS... MY BAR TAB WAS OVER TWO GRAND THIS EVENING AND I ONLY HAD 5 BEERS.
I stopped dead in my tracks and clasped my hand over my mouth, was GQ seriously texting me? With all the drinking we had done I'd almost forgotten all about him. I blushed

remembering how good he smelled and how nice my body felt when he'd wrapped his solid arms around me.

GQ?!?!

WHO?

LOL, GQ...I NEVER CAUGHT YOUR NAME AND YOU RESEMBLED A GQ MODEL, SO IT STUCK.

HA! WELL THEN, YES, GQ. WHY DON'T YOU COME DOWNSTAIRS AND MEET ME FOR A DRINK, I'M HEADED TO THE BAR.

A drink, was he serious? I was still drunk off my ass, there was no way I could drink anymore, not without potentially killing myself in the process. But there was just something about him that made me throw on my flip flops and saunter to the elevator. As I walked through the lobby, I quickly realized that I'd already changed into my pajamas and I was sporting yoga pants and a tank top, probably not the best outfit considering he'd last seen me in a dress so short my ass almost popped out, but what the hell, I was still half drunk, beyond exhausted, it was almost four in the morning, and I was pretty positive most of the hotel guests were already in bed.

"Hey there," he whispered, sneaking up behind me. I turned and was looking straight up into his eyes. Damn, he was gorgeous, I mean I'd realized it in the club, but now that we were out of the dark atmosphere I could actually see him, all of him. He towered over me, I was guessing he had to be pushing 6'5", his skin was perfectly tanned, he either lived at the beach or he was a frequent customer at the tanning salon. The five o'clock shadow that lingered on his jaw had come in just enough to make me wonder what it would feel like pressed against my neck.

"Hi," I said shyly, trying to avoid eye contact.

"How was that Patron?" He inquired, running his hand through his dark brown hair, giving me just enough time to catch a glimpse of his muscular stomach, as well as a trail of hair leading down south into his boxers. My cheeks instantly flushed red as tiny beads of sweat began to blossom on the back of my neck.

"Well, tonight it was a hit, but I'm sure tomorrow we'll all be cursing your name." He chuckled and looked at the time on his phone. "It looks like the bar is closed up for the night, but if you'd like we can go back to my room, they have the bar fully stocked?"

I knew this had the potential to get out of hand, but I figured it was the least I could do considering I'd forced him to pay for all of our very expensive liquor.

"Sure." I smiled and turned towards the elevators. He placed a hand on the small of my back and a shot ran straight up my spine, my body instantly covered in goose bumps. What was it about this man? It's like his mere touch rocked me to the core.

When he finally opened the door to his suite I was a nervous wreck. The tequila must have been wearing off. "Can I please have a shot, of anything?"

"More shots, how are you not passed out by now?"

"I'm not sure, but it doesn't really matter, can you just get me one, please?" He walked behind the bar and poured me a shot of Whisky. Oh man, this was not going to sit well, but I didn't care, I picked it up and slammed it back. My throat was already so numb I couldn't even feel the burn that I'm sure was lingering behind. I set the glass down and asked for one more.

"I don't think that is a good idea."

"Well, it's a good thing you aren't my boss, one more, now." I took the second shot and I knew I'd be so much more comfortable in about thirty seconds. I was positive all it would take was some added liquor courage to regain my earlier buzz.

"Here, drink this." He handed me a glass of water. Knowing full well that would kill my buzz I just left it there. "Ok, suit yourself, but don't be surprised if you are puking your guts out later tonight."

"Oh, I'm sure I can hold my own," I said, leaning across the bar, closer to his face. And there it was, my buzz was rearing its ugly head and I was getting bold all over again.

It only took four steps and he'd moved from behind the bar and both of his strong arms had been placed on either side of my hips. His face wasn't even an inch away from mine as I felt his breath wash over my lips. "I bet you can," he said in a throaty voice before his mouth slammed into mine.

I was completely caught off guard, and by the time I'd realized what was going on his strong hands were already gripping my ass and lifting me up around his waist. I grabbed fistfuls of his hair and devoured his mouth at the same rate he was taking mine. His tongue slipped past my lips and I let out a moan, arching my body closer to him. Before I knew it, I was pressed up against the wall and he was pulling my shirt over my head, his tongue tracing its way down my neck and over my collarbone. I couldn't control the movement of my hands, it was as if they were metal and his body was the magnet. I wanted nothing more than to touch every inch him, so I did.

He continued teasing my body as he carried me through the living room. My sports bra was tugged off of me as he sucked one of my breasts into his mouth. I gasped for air, trying to hold on tighter with my legs, since my head was flung back to open myself up further to his mouth, leaving me further off balance. His eyes gazed over my bare chest and up to meet mine, looking pleased with the moans that were escaping my throat. By the time we'd made it to the bedroom he had every ounce our clothing removed. They left a trail from the bar to the bed. Tossing me onto the bed he leaned in and took my mouth, biting my bottom lip, as I ran my nails down his shoulder blades pulling him further between my legs. The sound of foil ripped, and before I could offer my assistance he'd taken my body just as quickly as I'd given myself to him. From what I remembered, it was the most amazing orgasm I'd ever experienced. But what came next made me not want to even think about sex.

Chapter Three

I opened my eyes and the room was spinning. I was going to kill Addison for encouraging me to drink all of that tequila. I got out of bed and ran straight to the bathroom. I hated throwing up, but at that point I was willing to do whatever it took to rid myself of the liquor that was still lingering in my system. The bathroom seemed much bigger than I remembered, but at that very moment I couldn't care less about the size, all I was worried about was how quickly I could make it to the toilet. Just in the nick of time I dropped to my knees and began praying to the porcelain gods.

After twenty minutes of pure torture, I'd showered, brushed my teeth, and walked out of the bathroom ready to get back into bed and go to sleep. I pulled the covers back, so I could lie down and that's when I saw his naked body lying there, sprawled out in all of his gorgeous glory. My hands flew to my mouth and I whispered to myself, "Oh shit, you've got to be kidding me." My eyes darted along the floor looking for anything that resembled an article of my own clothing. I didn't see anything, so I ran into the living room and quickly grabbed the clothes I'd been wearing last night, which were scattered around the room, threw them on and ran straight for the door.

I couldn't believe I'd had a one night stand with GQ. Pacing in front of the elevator bank I couldn't help but replay last night's events in my head. How had I allowed myself to end up in a stranger's bed, what was I thinking? Clearly I wasn't, that was the problem. I'd let the liquor get the best of me and now I'd have to deal with the consequences. I leaned against the elevator wall breathing heavily, rambling a mile a minute to myself, like an idiot all the way to our floor, "Oh my gosh, I don't even know his name. It's official, I'm a slut. How could I be so stupid? To think I gave in so easily, I didn't even make him work for it. Sure, it was great, hell it was fan-freaking-tastic. But that doesn't change the fact that I just had my first official one night stand and I don't even know the guy's name. I'm sure Mom and Dad are so proud. Damn you, Reagan, get it together, everyone does it; at least you waited until you were twenty-seven and didn't cave at nineteen, like Addison had."

The bell chimed on our floor and the doors of the elevator opened, while I was still pacing the tiny space and talking to myself. An older gentleman's throat cleared and I was brought back to reality. *Wonderful, now the guests here think they're sharing a hotel with a lunatic.* "Oh! Excuse me," I shouted as I ran past him and straight to our penthouse suite.

Much to my surprise all of the girls were up, bearing bikinis, ready for our day at the beach. "Where in the hell did you run off to last night?" Addison screamed across the suite. "I've been calling you all morning!" She was standing there with her hands on her hips, looking like a pissed off mother who'd just found her teenager sneaking back into the house from the night before.

"Please stop screaming," I begged, "my head is pounding and I just woke up in bed with a man, oh, and did I mention I don't even know his name, just give me a minute to process and I'll get back to you."

"You WHAT?!" She was immediately at my side dragging me into our bedroom. If there was one thing Addison was more interested in than herself it was my sex life, or more like my lack thereof. She flung me onto the couch and plopped down right next to me. "You have got to tell me everything, right now."

"Look, I'm not even sure I remember anything. I was pretty toasted last night, no thanks to you and your damn tequila shots, all I know is he's here, in this hotel and we have to leave before he finds out what room we're in. I cannot run into him, ever." I leaned back against the couch and closed my eyes, hoping it would keep her from asking any more questions. No such luck.

"Are you kidding me, was it that terrible?"

I laughed, "Umm, not exactly, from what I do remember it was probably the best sex I've ever had in my entire existence." I blushed when I said it, granted it was only Addison, but I was still embarrassed.

"Then what in the hell are you hiding for? You should still be in that room with him getting ready for round two."

"No way," I screamed. "Look, guys like him probably have a different girl every night. I'm sure I did him a favor by leaving without waking him. Now, come on, let's go." I got up and moved as quickly as my aching body would let me, grabbing my things, and throwing them into my bag. Addison grabbed all of her luggage, tossed on her cover up and we went downstairs to check out. I'd put on my sunglasses and floppy hat to try and disguise myself, just in case GQ made his way to the lobby for whatever reason. I was casing the lobby of the hotel like a detective, and I think Addison was purposefully taking longer than needed in hopes of spotting him. Once we were in my SUV, and pulling out of the hotel parking lot, I felt like I could actually breathe again.

Addison was raking me over the coals about the details, but I really didn't have much to offer her, there wasn't much I remembered. "Look, you know I'm not like that, I don't just go hooking up with random guys wanting to have one night stands. I'm not sure what got into me last night, but it's over with and I just have to forget about it." I tried to focus on the road, but my head was still pounding. "Do you have any aspirin?" Addison dug through her giant purse and finally found a bottle of white pills and handed me two, luckily there was bottled water in the cup holder. I was going to need more than this to get through the day.

"Does he have your phone number?" she asked quietly.

"He won't call, trust me, he got what he wanted last night. Now, enough about me, this is your last Sunday as a single woman, let's focus on you." And that is exactly how we spent the rest of the day, baking in the scorching sun, drinking Bloody Marys.

Chapter Four

The next week was nothing but final wedding preparations, granted Addison had hired Tampa's best wedding planner, but there were still things she wanted taken care of herself, and as maid of honor it was my job to see all of it had been checked off of her list. From wedding ring pickups, to trips to and from the airport for family and friends, I seemed to be in charge of everything.

I was thankful; staying busy was keeping my mind off of the fact that GQ totally met my expectations, and had yet to contact me after our wild evening together. I know I had no reason to be, but I was furious.

While I was sitting at the airport stewing over GQ, and waiting on yet another flight, I called Addison. She answered the call, "Please tell me you are at the airport, Casey's aunt and uncle just landed and they will die if they have to wait for someone to pick them up."

"Oh come on, you know I'm never late, you've made me your bitch and I intend on fulfilling that position, but I just want to know why Casey's best man doesn't have to do any of this, shouldn't we be splitting all of the last minute to-do's?"

"Yeah right, you know how the guys are, they want as little to do with this stuff as possible. Casey told them the only thing they are responsible for is showing up sober the day of the wedding."

"Great, I'll be sure to thank Case when I see him. I've got to go; I think I've spotted the aunt and uncle, damn, for an old man he is a total knock out."

"Good genes, be nice to them, they're the Best Man's parents."

"Even more reason he should be helping me!" I exclaimed.

"Gotta run, have fun, I'll see you soon." She ended the call.

I jumped out of the car to greet Casey's uncle and aunt, "Mr. & Mrs. Conrad?"

"Yes, that's us," the older man said in a deep voice.

"Hi, I'm Reagan, Addison's best friend. It's so nice to meet the both of you." We all shook hands, and then I helped Mr. Conrad get their bags into the back of my SUV. Once their bags were packed into the back of the car, I jumped back into the driver's seat and headed towards Addison's parent's house.

"Aren't we going to The Bellevue?" Mr. Conrad asked.

"Yes, but first everyone is going to the Cartwright's for dinner, then I believe we'll all carpool back to the hotel."

"Oh good, I hope Colton will be there," said a tiny voice from the back seat. I looked into my rearview mirror; Mrs. Conrad looked like she was anticipating a long awaited homecoming.

"Colton?" I asked, looking to Mr. Conrad.

"Yes, our son, he lives here in Tampa. Hardly makes it home to see his parents, he's a very busy man. It will be good to see him, but I don't want you to go getting your hopes up, Candice, you know he'll probably only be available the day of the wedding." He said, looking into the back seat at his wife.

"Well, I hope he is there and you get to see him more than just at the wedding. I wish I could visit my parents." *Damn.* The words flew out before I could catch them and reel them back in.

"Do they not live in town?" Mr. Conrad asked.

"Well, they did, they passed a few years ago in an accident."

"Oh, I'm so sorry for your loss"

"Thanks, it was extremely hard at first, but it gets easier as time goes by. Anyway, I can't say that I've met Colton yet, but I'm sure he misses you all just as much as you miss him." Mrs. Conrad smiled at me from the back seat and the rest of the car ride was pretty silent. When we arrived at the Cartwright's I dropped Mr. & Mrs. Conrad off at the front door, then went to park my car.

I was finally done with all of my errands for the day and could relax with the rest of my family and friends. After running upstairs to my room – yes, after my parents passed Theo and Teresa Cartwright had taken me in and given me my own room in their house – and getting changed, I headed back downstairs to enjoy the evening.

Addison and Casey looked stunning amongst all of their friends and family. They were perfect for each other, both beautiful beyond description. She was tall and blonde and he was taller and blonder, their kids would definitely be super model material. Everyone was toasting champagne and sampling hor'dourves when I spotted Mrs. Conrad from across the room. I walked over to her and asked, "Have you seen Colton yet?"

She smiled and placed her hand on my arm, "Not yet, dear, but when I do, please remind me to introduce him to you. You know he's single?"

"Oh really," I laughed "I hadn't heard that, you'll have to introduce me to him when he arrives." I really wasn't interested in meeting anyone, in fact my mind was still all over

GQ, but Mr. and Mrs. Conrad seemed nice enough and I'm sure their son was just like them. So what the heck, besides, it was Thursday evening which meant it was almost a full week since I'd had my first one night stand and I still hadn't heard from him, I'm pretty sure that meant I wasn't going to. It was time to forget about him and move on, and what a perfect thing to do with Casey's mysterious cousin, Colton. If he looked anything like his father, I was sure he had to be gorgeous. I excused myself from Mrs. Conrad and enjoyed the rest of the evening.

By the time Friday evening rolled around Addison had run me ragged, I was sure the wedding planner had it easier than I did, and she was getting paid. Luckily, I'd just finished my last errand of the day and I was off to the spa to get my hair blown out for the rehearsal dinner. After my hair was finished, I swung by my house, got dressed, and headed straight for the church. Of all nights to be running late this was not it, Addison was going to kill me.

I barged into the church and Addison and Theo were standing at the end of the aisle, she looked panicked. *Shit. They had to start without me; at least my hair looks good.* I thought as I grabbed my fake bouquet from Addison, hugged and kissed her and Theo, and mouthed I'm sorry, I'm late to the both of them as I scurried down the aisle.

I don't think I'd even made it half way down the aisle when I glanced up to see how excited Casey looked and at that very moment I locked eyes on none other than GQ himself, he was standing right next to Casey. I stopped in my tracks as his eyes peered into mine. My heart was pounding out of my chest. Addison's mom, Teresa, whispered from the front pew, "Keep walking Reagan, you've got to make it all the way down the aisle." Thankful for her interruption, I regained my focus and continued walking down the aisle, all the while keeping my eyes sealed on GQ. From the looks of it he was just as stunned as I was. I made it to my spot front and center just as Addison and her dad finally began their descent down the aisle. I tried to keep focused on her, but I felt him glaring at me as they made their way towards us.

The rehearsal took forever and each time I'd position myself perfectly behind Addison she'd move and there he was staring straight back at me. When Pastor Bob announced that Casey may kiss the bride, Addison only allowed him her cheek, and everyone laughed as they applauded in excitement. I sighed with relief that it was finally over and began to bee-line it to the exit of the church, thankful Addison had enough faith in us to not have to practice the recessional back up the aisle. But before I could make it Mrs. Conrad stopped me and grabbed my hand, "Reagan, Colton is here. I would love for you to meet him, please let me introduce you."

"I'm sorry Mrs. Conrad, but I really have to step out for some fresh air, can we do this a little later?"

"No, ma'am, I insist, it will just take a moment. Wait right here while I go get him." I smiled at her as she hurried toward her son. Seconds later GQ and his mom were standing right in front of me as she introduced us. "Colton, this is Reagan, she is the maid of honor and Addison's best friend."

He stuck out his hand. "Pleasure to meet you, Reagan, my parents call me Colton, but everyone else calls me Cole."

I stuck out my hand to shake his and the instant our skin touched there it was, that same shock I'd felt the first night I'd met him. "Cole, it's nice to finally meet you, your mom and dad have told me so much about you."

Mrs. Conrad squealed and clapped her hands together. "I'm so excited to finally introduce the two of you. Weddings are such wonderful places for singles to meet."

"Mom, stop. I'm sure Reagan isn't interested in a relationship with anyone, she'd probably rather get what she wants out of a man and leave him in the middle of the night without any explanation."

"Colton Conrad, apologize to Reagan, right this instance,

I will not have you be so rude."

"No worries, Mrs. Conrad, I'm sure Cole is just referring to his own ways as opposed to mine. Cole, it was a pleasure meeting you, now if you'll both excuse me." I marched hastily away from the both of them as I heard tiny Mrs. Conrad ripping her son a new one.

Once outside, I walked around to the side of the church and went into full on panic attack mode. My heart was heaving out of my chest and my hands were trembling. How dare he talk to me like that in front of his mother? Damn it, I was so stupid, I'd fallen right into his trap, he played me for a fool and I'd fallen for it hook, line, and sinker. I leaned against the side of the church and tried to catch my breath. But it was next to impossible, that night just kept playing over and over in my head. What were the odds that my one night stand was none other than my best friend's future cousin? It must have taken me a half hour to get my heart rate back to normal when I realized I was one of the last ones at the church.

Pulling myself together, I heard Addison yelling my name, "Reagan! Where are you?"

I came around from the side of the church and she spotted me, "Why'd you run off?" She looked concerned.

"Sorry, I just got choked up seeing you and Casey. I needed some fresh air." She hugged me. There was no way I was going to fill her in on what had just happen, not the night before her wedding. "Go get your car and follow me and Casey, we've got to get to the restaurant, so everyone isn't waiting on us." I ran off to my SUV and jumped in, just as I started the engine my phone chimed.

WE NEED TO TALK.

Need to talk my ass! My fingers were going a mile a minute on the keypad.

I'M SORRY, BUT I HAVE NOTHING TO SAY TO YOU! I'LL BE CIVIL BECAUSE ADDISON IS MY BEST FRIEND AND I WANT NOTHING MORE THAN FOR HER TO HAVE A PERFECT WEDDING, BUT I DO NOT WANT TO TALK!

OH QUIT BEING A BRAT.

You have got to be kidding me, that didn't even deserve a response. I threw my phone on the passenger's seat next to me and kept my eyes focused on the road, avoiding anything that was coming through on my cell phone.

Dinner was brutal. Of course, Addison and Casey wanted their maid of honor and best man right by their side at all times, so I was forced to interact with Cole the entire evening, from sitting next to him at dinner, to taking pictures with him and his family. Every time he touched me, I cringed, but I was going to be the better person, I wasn't going to let him win. By the time dessert rolled around I was beyond ready to get as far away from Cole Conrad as possible. But I still couldn't, Addison insisted that we stay as long as the guys did because she didn't want to leave Casey.

It was tradition that the bride and groom spend their last night apart from each other, so, of course, Addison was going to stay until we absolutely had to leave. "Addison, we really need to go, you're going to have bags under your eyes tomorrow, just think how that will look in pictures."

"Come on," she leaned into me pouting her lips, "I hate being away from Case, just a few more minutes, please" she begged, scurrying over to Casey. Gosh they were irritating sometimes, they were inseparable and I was glad. I'd always hoped she get her knight and shining armor, but sometimes it made me want to gag.

"Why don't you have a shot of whiskey? Maybe that will calm your nerves, and you'll loosen up a bit." My body froze as Cole's breath caressed the side of my cheek and his hand traced the length of my arm.

I snapped my head around and looked up into his golden eyes, my breath instantly faltered. Damn this man. "I won't be needing anything to loosen me up, especially around you."

He smirked and cocked his head to the side. "I guess you're right, I've already seen you as loose as you're going to get." Before I knew it the palm of my hand was connecting with his face and the entire room fell silent. Luckily, all that was left was the wedding party. I'd have died had all of the Cartwright's and Conrad's still been there.

Casey walked up behind me and rested his hand on my back, "everything ok?"

I turned around to look up at my best friend's fiancé and I wanted to scream, No! Your cousin is an asshole! But instead I smiled and said, "Yes. Sorry, Case, I was just startled by your cousin, but I think he's okay." Casey looked towards his cousin, and Cole nodded his head. "Good, now if you'll excuse me I'm going to get back to my future wife." He kissed my cheek and rushed off towards Addison.

"What the fuck did you just slap me for?" Cole whispered, so we wouldn't draw any more attention to ourselves.

"I'm not some two bit hussy who goes around sleeping with people, and let me tell you, I loathe the day I ever crawled into your bed."

"Come on, Reagan, was it that bad?" No, it wasn't that bad, in fact it was probably one of the best nights of my life, from what I remembered, but I wasn't going to tell him that, not after he completely ignored me after the fact.

"I'm not doing this, Cole, not here, this night isn't about us. Let's just get through this evening and tomorrow and after that you can go back to ignoring me." I whipped myself around and went straight for Addison. "Come on, Bridezilla, we need to get you to bed, we have an early morning tomorrow."

Casey wrapped his arms tightly around her and held on for dear life. "Please, don't make her leave, can't I just take her home with me? No one will know."

"Absolutely not, it's bad luck. Besides, while you all are sleeping in tomorrow morning we'll be at the salon getting beautiful, now say goodbye, we have to go." Casey and Addison turned to each other and made out like two love struck teenagers without a care in the world. "Okay, okay, you don't want any hickies on your wedding day do you?" I grabbed Addison's arm and pulled her away.

She waved to Casey and yelled back to him, "I love you, baby, tomorrow you'll be my husband!"

"I love you, more, Mrs. Conrad!" We heard Case yell as we walked out the front door of the restaurant.

Both of us were laughing at their performance. "You two are so lame."

"We are not, we're just in love. Don't you worry, one day you'll find yourself someone just as special as Casey is to me. Who knows, maybe you and Cole will hit it off?"

"It'll be a cold day in hell." I said under my breath, trying to avoid that subject. There was no way I wanted Addison to know Cole was my GQ, she'd flip and we'd be up all night talking about it. Knowing her, she'd have us engaged and married by next weekend, just so she and I could finally really be family.

Chapter Five

"Get up! Get Up! Get Up! I'm getting married today!" Addison was shouting at the top of her lungs and jumping on my bed like a child.

I rolled over in bed to look at my phone and the time read 6:30 AM. "Ugh, go back to sleep, we don't have to be to the salon until 8:30."

"Who cares, this is the best day of my life and I can't sleep any longer and I need you to get your ass out of bed and celebrate with me." Clearly she didn't get enough sleep last night, but what could I do, she was right, it was the happiest day of her life. I forced myself to wake up and I climbed up on the bed, so I was standing face to face with her. We both began jumping on the bed and screaming like fools. We were laughing so hard the tears were pouring down our faces. I hugged her so tight.

"I'm so happy for you, you have no idea. You and Case are perfect for each other, and I cannot wait to see the two of you finally make it official today." She grabbed my hand and pulled us both down onto the bed, so we were lying side by side.

"Okay, I'm going to get sentimental here, so just bear with me for a second. Today is the happiest day of my life, but I want you to know none of this would've been possible without you. You knew Case long before I did, and it was your bright idea to introduce us. You're the sister I never had and I'm so grateful that we're celebrating this day together. There is no one else I'd rather have by my side than you. And one day, when you finally get your head out of your ass, you'll be waking me up at who knows what hour of the morning, so we can jump up and down on the bed and scream about the fact that you are marrying the man of your dreams."

I hugged my best friend so tight. And in that very instant a picture of Cole flashed through my head. "Okay, enough of the heavy, let's get this party started." I jumped out of bed, pulling Addison up with me. I had to get focused on something else, so I wasn't thinking about him. *He* was the last person I wanted to associate with marriage.

It hadn't taken much to get my mind off of Cole. Mimosas, a Swedish massage, hair and makeup, and I was in wedding la-la-land, right there with my best friend. "Reagan, you look stunning."

I looked in the mirror and smiled at myself, I looked great, but Addison was the belle of the ball. "I've definitely got nothing on you, Mrs. Casey Conrad." She was beaming as she critiqued every centimeter of the both of us in the full length mirror we were posing in front of.

"Can you believe that will be my real name in just a few hours?"

Of course, I could. Case had fallen head over heels on their very first date. "Of course I can." I said, hugging her. Oh man, this day was going to get emotional, I could already tell. "Okay, okay, no tears, we don't want to ruin our make-up, and you don't want the first thing Casey sees when you are walking down the aisle towards him to be raccoon eyes."

She laughed. "You're right, no more crying."

After spending the morning at the salon, we'd all packed into the limo and headed towards the church to finish getting ready. Addison had us on a tight schedule, there was no way we could be late, and she was beyond ready to finally become Mrs. Casey Conrad. The bridal room was packed with bridesmaids, family members, photographers, and hair and make-up artist in case we needed touch ups. We were all buzzing around the room getting ready, while enjoying the day together.

"Reagan!" Addison screamed from across the bridal suite.

I was at her side in an instant. "What's wrong?" I asked, worried.

"Oh, nothing's wrong, I just wanted to see if you could take this gift over to Case. I got him cufflinks, and I want to make sure he wears them during the ceremony."

"Of course, I'll take them, and I'll bring back a mental picture of how handsome he looks." I grabbed the perfectly wrapped box and card, then walked out of the room towards the groom's suite.

Knocking on the door, I heard loud laughter and commotion. I let myself in just as the guys were lifting shot glasses to their lips, a half empty bottle sitting in the middle of all of them. "And here I thought the only rule you all had was no drunken groomsmen?" I giggled.

All of the guys turned to me and grinned as they set their empty shot glasses down. "You know we won't get drunk, we're just celebrating." Casey had the cutest smirk on his face as he stood up and came over to hug me. "Reagan, if you look this beautiful I can't even begin to imagine what my future wife looks like."

"She's stunning, Case, you're definitely the luckiest man alive." He released me and I handed him the box and card. "This is from Addison. She wanted me to bring them to you, so you could wear them during the ceremony."

He opened the card and laughed at what she'd written him. When he opened the box you could tell he was taken back a bit. He pulled the cufflinks out of the box and looked up at me. "These are my great grandfather's cufflinks. He wore them the day he married my great grandmother, right before he shipped off to war." You could tell he was surprised and thrilled at the same time. Addison had done well.

"They're perfect, Case." I said, taking them out of his hands and putting them on for him. He held out his arms for everyone to see. "Well" I said, adjusting his tie "you all look very handsome and as much as I'd love to sit around and admire that, I have a bride to get back to." I hugged Case once more and turned to walk out the door. As I opened the door to leave the room I ran smack into a rock hard chest, and muscular arms wrapped around me to steady my wobbly body.

"Hey there, little lady." I didn't even have to look into his eyes to know who had their arms wrapped around me.

"Excuse me, Cole, I've got to get back to Addison" I said, pushing him off of me, trying to avoid eye contact.

"Wait," he demanded, grabbing my shoulders and spinning me around, so I was facing him. I was staring up into those eyes as he looked me over from head to toe, his scent filling my nose. "You're beautiful, Reagan."

"Says the best man who probably just wants to get laid by the maid of honor tonight."

His eyes filled with rage and he stepped in closer, forcing me up against a wall as his right hand came around the back of my neck, while his left leaned against the wall holding his entire weight centimeters from my body. I could feel the heat radiating off of him. My mouth fell slightly open as I looked up into his eyes. "I don't need to give compliments to get laid, Reagan." My name on his tongue sent shivers down my spine. "But, if that's what it'd take to get you back in my bed, I'd never stop." I stood there, gawking at him, not knowing what to say. He leaned in, kissed the side of my cheek, and closed my open mouth with his finger. "You're going to catch flies that way." He grinned and left me standing there as he walked into the groom's suite and closed the door behind him. *Damn him.* I thought as I stomped away.

Once back in the room with the girls it seemed things began moving at full speed. We were all getting our jewelry on, bouquets in order and getting ready to begin our walks down the aisle. Theo came and hugged both Addison and me. "You're both beautiful beyond words."

I smiled at him. "I'll give you two a minute alone." I walked out into the foyer where all of the girls were lined up and made sure that everything was in order. The wedding planner was sending the first bridesmaid down the aisle as Addison and her dad emerged out of the room. "You both ready?" I asked them when they got to my side.

"Yes" they said in unison. We all smiled. Just then the wedding planner shuffled me into line, as I was next. The music was playing, I held my bouquet in place and I began my journey towards the front of the church. Case looked so handsome. He was grinning from ear to ear. I could tell he was looking past me to try and catch a glimpse of Addison. *No such luck buddy, you've got two flower girls and a ring bearer to get through first.* I thought to myself. As I passed Casey and stood next to Addison's spot I tried to focus on everything but Cole. I hadn't even looked at him as I was making my way towards the front. The kids were next and then the bridal march began.

Everyone stood up and the doors swung open. I'd already seen Addison, so my first reaction was to look at Casey. He was beaming at the sight of his soon to be wife. I looked back to Addison; she was practically floating down the aisle, until she reached Casey. Theo kissed Addison's cheek, shook Casey's hand, and gave his daughter away to her future husband. The ceremony was lovely. It took everything I had to not cry throughout the entire thing. I was just so elated for my best friend. When Pastor Bob announced them husband and wife the place erupted in applause and cheers. I tilted my head, grinning as I watched them have their first kiss as husband and wife.

I glanced up to try to keep the tears in check, and saw Cole staring hard into my eyes. It caught me off guard. I'd been trying to avoid looking at him throughout the entire ceremony. He flashed a smile at me and I felt my stomach summersault. I quickly straightened back up and handed Addison's bouquet to her as she and Case made their way up the aisle together. Cole met me in the middle and I linked my arm in his, fighting the tingle I felt upon touching his body. "You know you're the most gorgeous woman here today."

"Shut.Up, Cole." I said through gritted teeth, trying to maintain my smile as we made our way towards the back of the church.

Addison and Casey were still kissing when we made it to them. When they finally unlocked lips, I got to hug and congratulate the both of them before everyone else got their attention. We spent the next hour taking pictures as guests made their way to The Bellevue, where the reception would take place.

The photographer must have thought it was opposite day, because he was doing exactly the opposite of what I wanted. Every time I'd move to the opposite side of where Cole was for a picture, he'd grab me and pull me back towards him. It was really starting to aggravate me. Even on the ride over to the hotel he had to sit next to me in the limo. Case was toasting to everyone on the ride over, "Here's to spending the rest of my life with my beautiful wife. To my best man, who has always been there for me and to Reagan, if it weren't for you introducing me and Addison we may have never met." He went on and we all took a drink as he finished.

But before I could get my champagne down my throat Addison interjected "And here's to Reagan and Cole, you two look great together, who knows, maybe we'll be celebrating your wedding next!" I choked on my champagne as it flew out of my mouth. My eyes were bulging out of my head. Cole laughed and Addison shot me a wink, but it was attached to a devilish grin.

"What the hell was that about?" I whispered to her as she climbed out of the limo. "Case and I have a no secrets policy and apparently while him and Cole were having drinks last night you came up."

"I came up?" I parroted, blushing.

"Yea, you. And don't give me that innocent look, Case told me Cole's the guy you slept with the night of my bachelorette party." She was grinning from ear to ear.

"Shit, Addison, I'm sorry I didn't tell you. I was trying to wait until after you got back from your honeymoon."

"That's ok, I forgive you, well, as long as you agree to the date me and Case are going to set up."

My heart stopped. "No, no way, I'm not going on a date with him. It was a one night stand and that's it. You aren't playing match maker with me again." I was still getting over slime ball Sam from the last time Addison had set me up on a blind date.

"Oh yes, you are. I already talked to Case about it, we both think it's a great idea." There was no winning with her, I knew it was best to just agree and get it over with. Addison was a force to be reckoned with. I knew her well enough to know once she had her mind set on something she wouldn't stop until she'd achieved her goal.

"Fine, I'll agree, but only because I'm sure Cole won't."

She laughed, giving me a very un-reassuring squeeze. "You know how persuasive I can be, especially when it comes to getting you settled down." I groaned as we all walked into the hotel together.

The DJ announced all of the wedding party, followed by Addison and Casey upon our arrival. They walked into the reception hall and made their way to the dance floor as the music began playing for their first dance. We all sat down to watch from the head table, of course, Cole's name card was right next to mine. Case and Addison were spinning around the dance floor, completely in love with each other while we all watched. As the song ended Case dipped Addison and kissed her lips before handing her off to her father.

Chapter Six

Tears began to spill down my cheeks as I watched Addison and Theo twirl around the dance floor to Heartland's *I Loved Her First*. I was so happy for her in this moment, but I was also hurting so badly inside, knowing I'd never get the chance to dance with my own father at my wedding. It was something I'd dreamt about since I was a little girl; my Dad and I would practice dancing to our favorite song, Lionel Richie's *Ballerina Girl*, whenever it would come on the radio.

Cole leaned over and wrapped his arm around my shoulder, pulling me closer to him. My body stiffened as hard as a statue. "My mom told me about your parents. I'm so sorry, Reagan. I know this has got to be difficult for you." He had no idea. I'd never get to share this special moment with my parents, my heart was breaking into a million pieces as that realization came crashing down upon me. And for that moment I forgot about the fact that I was still utterly pissed off at him and let him comfort me. When he felt my body relax he held me even tighter into him. I laid my head on his shoulder, tears still slipping down my face as he rubbed my arm. I stayed there throughout the entire song, eyes closed imagining my dad spinning me around the dance floor.

The song finally ended and the room erupted in applause, there wasn't a dry eye in the house, so luckily I didn't look fully out of place. I tugged myself out of my daydream just as the DJ called the entire wedding party to the dance floor. Great, I was going to have to dance with him. Cole stood up, reached for my hand and led me to the dance floor. "I'm sorry their dance made you so upset." He said lifting my chin, so I was looking into his golden eyes.

"It's no big deal, don't worry about it, I'll be fine." He pulled my body even closer to his as we swayed from side to side. "You aren't a superhero, Reagan, quit acting like you don't have any emotions."

"I'm not trying to be a superhero, it's just a stupid dance. My dad didn't even like to dance, so I probably would have had to nix it anyways." *Can we please not talk about this right now.* I looked away from him, trying to hold back the tears, knowing that was so far from the truth.

Cole pulled me closer into his massive build, as if that was even possible as he rested his head atop of mine. "Even if your dad didn't dance, there's no way he'd miss out on dancing with you on your wedding day. There wouldn't be a man in the room who wouldn't want to dance with you." I let out a chuckle as he swayed our bodies back in forth, inhaling the scent that I'd still yet to figure out. Arguing with him was getting exhausting, so I just left it alone.

The wedding ended perfectly as fireworks lit up the night's sky over the water, it was beautiful and everyone had a wonderful time. As Casey and Addison were preparing to climb into their vintage white Rolls Royce they pulled both Cole and I to the side. "Cole, I need you to do me a favor while we're away, I want you to take my best friend out on a date, wine and dine her heart out. Anything she wants, do it. And if she asks you to take her to a fast food restaurant and call it a night I want you to call me immediately! You understand?"

He laughed and shook his head. "You got it boss."

"And you," she said pointing her perfectly manicured finger in my face. "I want you to enjoy yourself. Maybe not as much as the last time the two of you were together, but nonetheless, have a good time, relax and get to know him. Don't let his playboy reputation scare you. I know he's a good guy and he'll treat you right, because if he doesn't, Case will kick his ass, and so will I."

I smiled and pulled her into a hug. "Quit telling us what to do and get your ass to the airport, you're killing poor Case. He's ready to consummate this marriage, now quit making him wait!" We all laughed, and they hugged us both goodbye, waving out the back of the window towards everyone as they drove away.

"Well, you heard her, as much as I repulse you, it looks like there's no other choice but to go on a date with me." I rolled my eyes, ignoring him, and walked back into the reception towards the bar. Ordering a glass of wine and taking it back to the head table I sat down to rest. Luckily, Cole was grabbed by one of his little cousins and drug out onto the dance floor. I enjoyed watching the two of them, especially the 'save me glances' he shot my way every time the little girl made him spin her around in circles.

The reception hall was empty of almost all the guests when Cole finally made it back to his seat. Falling into his chair beside me, he lifted his beer towards his lips and took a long sip. "Well, it looks like the evening is wrapping up here, any chance you're interested in joining me for a few drinks in my room after everyone clears out?"

"No, thank you, I'd rather not go through that again."

He leaned his head to the side and cleared his throat. "I'm sorry, what is it that you went through that was so bad the last time you had drinks in my room?"

"Umm, let's see, we had amazing sex and then I never heard from you again. I think I'd rather spare myself the heartache and just go home and sleep in my own bed this time."

He placed his hand on the back of my chair and leaned in, so he was eye level with me, the rage was back in his eyes "I'm not sure why you're making me out to be the bad guy here, Reagan, you're the one who disappeared. In the real world when someone sneaks out in the middle of the night that's usually an indication that they don't want a follow up call." His words hit my chest like a ton of bricks and I took a sharp breath in as he continued, "You really need to get off of your high horse, if anything I should be the one who is pissed off at you, not the other way around. You're the one who walked out on me, just remember that." He stood up, grabbed his jacket off the back of my chair, and stormed out of the room. *Shit. He was right, we could have avoided all of this had I stuck around, or even woke him up to say goodbye.*

Theo and Teresa were supervising the collection of gifts as I made my way towards the exit. "You leaving, honey?" Teresa asked as she pulled me into a hug.

"Yes, I hope you don't mind. I know there are still a few people left, but I'm exhausted and just want to get home and into bed."

"Not at all," she assured me, holding me at arm's length, "you were such a huge help through all of this. We cannot thank you enough. Now, go home and get some rest." She hugged me again, as did Theo. I grabbed my clutch and headed towards the door, passing the hotel bar on the way out. Cole was sitting at the bar drinking a beer by himself. I stopped and looked in towards him grabbing my phone and sending him a quick text.

I'M SORRY.

He pulled his phone out of his pocket, looked at my text and set it down on the bar next to him, without response as he ran his hands through his hair. *Perfect, you've done it again, Reagan.* I thought to myself as my heart fell to the pit of my stomach. Trying to avoid the embarrassment of possibly being seen by him, I high tailed it to my car and headed home.

Chapter Seven

The weekend quickly passed and I was getting back into the swing of things at the office. I had put a huge dent in my inbox, when my assistant walked into my office and set a package on my desk. I opened the box and out fell a pair of sunglasses, a beach towel, and a bikini, along with a note.

Here are just a few things I've picked up at our resort. Consider going to the beach with Cole on your date. I know how much you love tanning, and the bikini is Brazilian cut, so he'll have a perfect view of your ass. You can thank me later.

Love and miss you. -Mrs. Casey Conrad

I had to laugh, leave it up to Addison to send me a bikini that looked three sizes too small. I suppose it's time I live up to my end of the deal, I thought. Closing my office door I pushed the speaker phone button and dialed Cole's number. It rang twice, and then went to voicemail. "Did he just ignore me?" I asked myself, thinking out loud. Fine, if he won't answer his cell, I'll call his office. "Shit!" I didn't have his office number, so I took to Google. I entered Colton Conrad, Tampa, FL into the search engine and an office number came up for Conrad Developers, LLC.

I dialed the number and a woman answered the phone, "Conrad Developers, this is Heather, how may I assist you?" Her voice was too perky.

"Hi, Heather, this is Reagan Larson. I'm looking to speak with Cole Conrad, if he's available?"

"One moment, while I check, please," she put me on hold and classical music played into the phone. I leaned back in my chair as I waited. The music stopped and the perky voice was back on the phone with me, "I'm sorry Ms. Larson, Mr. Conrad is unavailable at the moment, may I take a message?"

"No thank you, I'll just try again later." And I hung up. Instantly I grabbed my phone and sent him a text.

GIVE ME A CALL WHEN YOU GET A MINUTE, PLEASE.

I hadn't even set my phone down when it vibrated in my hand.

REALLY BUSY THIS WEEK, YOU'LL HAVE TO CALL MY ASSISTANT AND MAKE AN APPOINTMENT.

An appointment, was he out of his mind? I wasn't one of his clients. Without thinking twice, I pulled up his office address; it was downtown, only three blocks away from my building. I grabbed my purse and stormed out of my office, past my assistant, as I yelled over my shoulder, "Call all of my afternoon appointments and reschedule I have to take care of something and I'm not sure how long I'll be."

I ripped through the lobby and down the street, towards his building. The elevators opened and I stepped out into a grand lobby. The receptionist greeted me before I even arrived at her desk, "Good afternoon, ma'am. Welcome to Conrad Developers, how may I assist you?" There was that way too perky voice.

"Heather?" I asked, cocking my head to the side. "I'm here to see Cole Conrad, would you let him know he has a visitor?"

Her eyes looked confused as she checked his calendar on her computer. "I'm sorry, I don't see anything on his calendar, do you have an appointment?"

"No, but I'm sure he'll see me, just let him know Reagan Larson is here, would you."

She picked up her telephone and waited for an answer, "Hello, Mr. Conrad, you have someone here to see you." She waited for his response, "well, no there is nothing on your calendar, but she says you'll see her regardless...yes, her name is Ms. Larson...okay, I'll send her back, thank you." I smiled and walked past Heather as she shouted, "last door on your left!"

The office door was closed. I took a deep breath wondering what I was going to say when I walked in, but I guess it was a little late for that now wasn't it. I turned the handle and opened the door. I stepped into a giant corner office with floor to ceiling windows. Cole was in his chair behind a grand mahogany desk that looked big enough to seat eight people, perfect, he was on the phone. I stood there as he peered into my eyes. *Shit, why in the hell was I here, this was a mistake.* He pointed to the chair in front of his desk, but I was too nervous to sit, so I placed my purse in the chair and walked to the window, looking out over the city.

After a few minutes he'd ended his phone call and cleared his throat to get my attention. "So, what brings you to my office?" I whipped around and walked towards his desk, placing both hands on top of it as I leaned over it and looked him square in the eyes. "I wouldn't do that if I were you, you've seen where it will get you," he said in a deep voice.

I quickly stood and crossed my arms over my chest. "You want me to make an appointment to talk to you!" I exclaimed.

He leaned back in his chair and put his hands behind his head. He was the epitome of perfect. His crisp white button down shirt hugged his muscular frame just right, as his tie hung loosely around his neck paired with the top button of his undone collar. "Yes, I'm busy. Usually if someone needs to see me that is what they do, they call my assistant and make themselves an appointment."

"Oh, so I'm just like the rest of them, I need to make an appointment to see you? You know what, this was a mistake, I shouldn't have even come here. I'm sorry I wasted your time." I turned to walk towards the door when I heard hands slam against the desk. I quickly shot a glance over my shoulder at Cole. He was standing there running a hand through his hair.

"Damn it, Reagan, what do you want from me?"

I stood there stunned for a minute, since I hadn't really even asked myself that question yet. "I...I'm not sure, I just thought, well, we told Addison we'd go out and I guess I just figured we should probably get it over with before they get back." I stammered, practically tripping over my words.

"So that's it, you just want to go on our date, so we can get it over with?"

"Well, no, that's not what I meant." I trailed off, walking back towards the window, letting a sigh escape my throat. His footsteps thumped across the hardwood floors as he made his way over to me. I could feel the heat from his body while I watched his shadow approach in the glare of the window. His hands rested on my shoulders and the hairs on the back of my neck stood up. I relaxed into his hands and leaned back onto his chest, his fingers tracing their way down my arms and now gripping my hips as he pulled me closer to him.

"What do you want, Reagan, I'm not a mind reader, you've got to tell me?"

I took in a deep breath, it was now or never, if I waited I might chicken out. "You," I whispered, relieved that I'd finally said it. His hands left my hips and he walked away. *Crap, I knew this was a mistake, I shouldn't have admitted anything.* And then I heard his office door close, followed by the twist of the lock and before I knew it he was behind me again.

I turned around and looked up into those golden eyes. They looked as if they were smiling back at me. I lifted my trembling hands up to caress both sides of his face. "I want you, Cole. I've wanted you from the minute you touched me in the bar the night of Addison's bachelorette party." I pushed him back onto his chair and climbed on top of his lap, straddling him as I entwined my fingers into his hair. His eyes darkened and I grazed my tongue along the side of his jaw. "Is this ok?" I whispered into his ear, tugging his earlobe with my teeth. He moaned into my neck and I took that as a yes. A smile spread across my face as I continued to work my way from one side of his jaw to the other. Kissing his neck, I loosened his tie enough to slip it over his head. His hands had pulled my blouse out of my slacks and he had laced his arms up my back and over my shoulders.

I couldn't take it anymore, I wanted, no, needed to taste his mouth. I pulled his face closer to mine and pressed my lips to his as hard as I could. One of his arms wrapped around my waist. His other hand grabbed a fistful of my hair and tilted my head back, so he could control the intensity of our kiss. His lips ravaged mine like he'd been waiting his entire life to taste them, it was intoxicating. I could hardly catch my breath when he slipped his tongue into my mouth. And just as my hands were working their way down each button of his shirt, there was a knock on the door.

"Colton, are you in there?" We both froze. *Where had I heard that voice before?*

"Shit, it's my mom."

"Oh.My.Gosh." I jumped off of his lap and tried to straighten my clothes, I was tucking my blouse back into my pants faster than he pulled it out. I ran over to the window to try and see my reflection, bad idea, my hair was all over the place and my lips were swollen and bright red.

"Where's my tie?" he whispered, so no one would hear us. I ran back over to his chair and looked around and spotted it on the ground. I picked it up and handed it to him. He slipped the tie over his neck and began to tighten it.

"I cannot believe your mother is on the other side of the door. This is going to be so embarrassing." I bemoaned, adjusting every part of me that seemed out of place.

Cole grabbed the sides of my face. "Baby, calm down, we'll just tell her you were here for a meeting." He kissed my lips and I felt light headed. How could this man make me feel so many different things in such a short amount of time? He left me standing there as he opened the door and greeted his mother. "Mom, I wasn't expecting you, today," he said pulling her tiny frame into a hug. "Oh, I know, sweetie, but I was in the neighborhood and since your father and I are leaving tomorrow I thought I'd come by one last time." She clasped his hand as she walked further into his office. "I was thinking you could come over for dinner tonight... Oh, Reagan, I didn't realize you were in here." She said with a grin on her face. "How are you, darling?"

I walked over to her and she wrapped me in a hug, squeezing me extra tight. "I'm well, and yourself?"

"Oh just wonderful, I was just asking Cole if he'd like to join me and his father for dinner this evening, we'd love to have you come along as well, if you aren't busy." I looked to Cole in a panic, I wasn't sure what to say.

He smiled at me and nodded his head. "I'd love to join you for dinner, assuming Cole will be attending, that is?" We both looked to him.

He smiled and said, "Of course."

"Perfect, then we'll see the two of you tonight, let's say 7p.m. Oh, and Cole, be sure to clean up before you leave your office," she said walking towards the door, "you've got lipstick all over your collar." And with that she disappeared down the hallway.

I instantly turned bright red and sunk into the chair next to me. Cole was leaning against the wall. "Busted," laughing, he sauntered towards the chair I was sitting in. Reaching for my hands he pulled me out of the chair and into his arms. "Just so you know, tonight doesn't count as our date."

"Oh no?" I asked, grinning as I draped my arms around his neck.

"No, technically my mother invited you, so I still get to take you out after this."

"I suppose we'll see about that," I whispered as I wiggled my way out of arms and over to my purse. I grabbed my bag and headed for the door as he followed me past the lobby towards the elevator banks. I stood there with him inches behind me as I awaited the elevator.

Upon its arrival, I stepped in and he grabbed the doors before they could close. "Text me your address and I'll swing by and pick you up at 6:45." I nodded and waved goodbye as the doors closed between us. *Great,* I thought. *I've got three hours to find an outfit.*

Chapter Eight

"Perfect." I complimented myself as I modeled my outfit in the mirror. I'd swung by my favorite boutique in Hyde Park and grabbed a little black dress that clung flawlessly to my curves. My six inch black stilettos made my legs look longer than they were. I was thrilled I'd be that much closer to Cole's face, thanks to the heels. I glanced down at my watch and it was 6:43p.m., just enough time to finish off my makeup with bright red lipstick as the doorbell rang.

"Coming!" I hollered, running across the hardwood floors towards the front door. Pulling the curtains aside, I saw Cole standing on my front porch. "SON OF A ….. ugh," I yelled way too loud.

He must have heard me through the door because his instant reply was, "What's wrong?" I leaned against the door with a loud thud. "Reagan, what's wrong, open the door."

"I can't," I said, frustrated.

"Why not?" I looked out the window again. Yep, he was still standing there in a light blue oxford with the sleeves rolled up his forearms, khaki shorts, boat shoes, and a pair of aviators. Even the top two buttons of his shirt were undone.

He looked too good to be true and I looked like an overdressed idiot.

"Can you just give me five minutes?" I asked, hitting my head against the door.

"No, open up. We're going to be late. We need to go." I didn't want to open the door out of pure embarrassment, but I did anyway, looking anywhere but in his eyes when I did. "Oh, wow..." He stammered, caught off guard.

"I know, I look like an idiot." I grumbled, hanging my head.

He stepped closer towards me and lifted my chin with his finger. "You look beautiful. A little over dressed for dinner, but nonetheless, absolutely stunning."

I flushed at his comment, but groaned at the fact that I had gone all out and here he was casual as ever. "Come in while I change." I turned on my heels and stormed off to my bedroom, unzipping my dress in the process. Heavy footsteps thumped down the hallway entering my bedroom just as I'd stepped out of my dress. I was standing there, frozen in surprise, in nothing but a black lace matching bra and panty set and my stilettos, watching Cole's reflection in my full length mirror. He approached me, his eyes running over my body, taking every inch in as he slowly moved closer towards me, placing both of his strong hands on my bare hips, like he was trying to keep me from disappearing. "Out there, what you were wearing, that was stunning, but this, you, right here, just like this, damn babe, there are no words for this." He leaned in and kissed my neck, his hands tightening on my hips, pulling my backside against his crotch.

My knees went weak and I had to focus on keeping myself from toppling over. He trailed light kisses from my neck to my bare shoulder, his right hand made its way over my belly, slipping a finger underneath the top of my lace panties. I moaned as my head fell back onto his shoulder. "As much as I'd love to continue this, we've got to get to dinner with your parents." I said, almost out of breath, grabbing his hand and returning it back to my waist.

A throaty laugh escaped his lips and he released his grip on my hips pushing me towards the closet. "If you intend on getting out of here without me removing the rest of your clothes I suggest you get your ass dressed, because my willpower is almost gone."

I smiled at him and ran into my closet laughing. I grabbed a sundress and threw it on, then exchanged my six inch heels for a pair of wedge sandals. Grabbing a matching clutch, I switched my necessities over from my purse. Leaving the closet, I skipped over to him and took his hand. "You ready, Mr. Conrad?"

"Not ready for dinner, more like ready to stay here and get you out of that dress." Shaking my head I giggled and tugged him towards the front door.

"Maybe we can come back here for dessert." I winked at him over my shoulder.

Cole pulled up to the valet when we arrived at the The Bellevue. "Good evening, Mr. Conrad." The valet attendant greeted when Cole beat him to open my door.

"They know you by name, huh, frequent customer?" I asked looking up into his magnificent eyes.

He smiled and took my hand, leading me towards the lobby. "You could say that."

Cole's father opened the door when we arrived at their suite. "Good evening, son. Reagan, it's so nice to see you, again."

"You, too, Mr. Conrad," I replied, leaning in to hug him.

"Please, call me Harrison." I smiled and stepped into the suite. It was beautiful, very similar to what I remembered of Cole's suite the first night I met him. The windows overlooked the crisp blue water, giving a beautiful backdrop to our dinner. The grand dining room set off to the side, the table fully prepared for a dinner party. Mrs. Conrad came out from the dining room to greet us with a glass of wine and a Yuengling in her hands for Cole and me.

"Hello, darlings, we're so glad you could join us for supper." She kissed both our cheeks, passing our drinks off to each of us. Cole and his dad were talking as Mrs. Conrad shooed them away. "You boys go relax in the study, while Reagan and I enjoy a glass or two of wine.

Cole placed his hand on the small of my back leaning into my ear to ask, "You going to be okay?" I nodded, smiling and he kissed my cheek. "She's harmless, I promise," he said as he walked away with his father.

"Is there anything I can help you with?" I asked, looking to Mrs. Conrad. "Not at all, dear. I just know Harrison needed to speak with Cole and I didn't want him interrupting our dinner with business. Now, why don't we go enjoy the balcony while the staff finishes setting the table." *Staff?* I thought to myself as I followed her out onto the balcony.

I took a deep breath, the familiar smell of saltwater filled my nose. The wind whipping around relaxed me. I wasn't nervous to be around his parents, but considering he and I had finally just decided to be nice to each other earlier this afternoon I wasn't fully comfortable in the situation either. You usually don't "meet the parents" until you've spent some time in a relationship with someone, and Cole and I weren't anywhere even close to a relationship, yet.

Wanting to break the silence I sat down on an oversized plush white pillow top couch, took a sip of wine for courage, and spoke, "This suite is beautiful, and the view…this sunset is going to be incredible."

"Oh, isn't it wonderful. Cole was so kind, designing the suite just for us, making sure we had the best view."

"Designed the suite, what do you mean?"

"Cole," she said like I should have known exactly what she was talking about. I tried to cover up my lack of knowledge by taking a sip of wine, but my confused eyes must have given it away. "This hotel, it was Cole's first project when he started his development company. It's what brought him to Florida. He's built dozens more since, but this was his first and his favorite, so he was sure to build out two special suites, one for us and one for him, since this is where he lives, Reagan."

I leaned back on the couch, pouring the remaining wine down my throat. *He owns this hotel, what the hell, no wonder Addison had all of her parties here. How had I not put two and two together?*

"More wine?" she asked, holding the bottle towards my glass.

"Please" I whispered, still taking it all in.

I must have looked like a crazy person staring at the water, because Mrs. Conrad came and sat next to me and grabbed my hand, bringing me out of my trance. "Reagan, is everything ok?"

"Yes, I'm sorry. I just didn't know, Cole hadn't mentioned it to me, so I guess I'm just surprised. I didn't realize he was so established."

"Oh, he is, Reagan, he has worked so hard to build his company and he has had success upon success. We are so proud of him, but we're worried, too. We want him to find a wonderful woman who will love him for him, not for all of this. Harrison and I are just so thrilled the two of you are together. The minute we met you, we both agreed you were perfect for our son."

I stood up and walked to the railing of the balcony, had his mother really just laid that on me? I turned and looked at her sitting there smiling up at me and I hated what I was about to tell her. "I'm so sorry, Mrs. Conrad, but I'm afraid you've gotten the wrong impression. Cole and I aren't together, well, I mean, it's just, he and I are complicated. I just don't want you and Mr. Conrad to get your hopes up, because I'm not even sure I know what this is."

She took a sip of her wine and got up to stand beside me,

placing her hand on my shoulder. "Oh, honey, you may be confused because it's new, but trust me when I tell you this, my son has had a lot of women and I've never seen him look at any of them the way he looks at you." I sucked in a breath of air as her words kept repeating themselves in my head.

"Would you excuse me, please?" I asked briskly walking away towards the restroom.

Closing the door behind me I sat down on the edge of the giant tub and put my head between my knees. *No panic attacks, Reagan, not now, not while you're here with all of them, get it together!* Catching my breath I stood up and began to pace the bathroom, "Harmless, my ass," I whispered to myself, "she's not harmless, she's crazy. What in the hell does she mean she's never seen him look at anyone that way? How was he even looking at me? I've got to get out of here, I shouldn't be here." Still pacing the bathroom floor I racked my brain for an excuse. *Got it, work, use work, and just tell them you had an emergency. Better yet, leave first, then text Cole.*

I slowly opened the bathroom door and peeked out of it, there was no one in sight and I had a clear shot to the front door. As quietly as I could I tiptoed from the bathroom to the front door, opening it as quickly as possible. I ran into the hallway, lightly closed the door behind me, and jumped on the first elevator I could catch. For whatever reason luck just happened to be working in my favor tonight, a cab sat outside of the hotel lobby. I jumped in and gave him my office address when he drove off.

Chapter Nine

I HAD TO RUN, PLEASE APOLOGIZE TO YOUR PARENTS FOR ME. THERE WAS AN EMERGENCY AT THE OFFICE THAT I HAD TO HANDLE ASAP.

I set the phone down next to me in the cab, ignoring the driver trying to engage in small talk. Staring out the window, I wondered what in the hell I'd just done. The sudden ringing of my phone scared the crap out of me. Cole's name was flashing across my screen. I sighed heavily, pressing the ignore button, not ready to explain to him why I left. The cab driver dropped me off at my office and I swiped my pass card up to the twenty-third floor.

The office was pitch black, since everyone had already gone home for the evening. I flipped the lobby lights on and walked into my office, collapsing into my chair. I argued with myself over my hasty exit. "Why did you leave, you idiot, she wasn't asking you to marry her son. She was only filling you in on an observation. And why are you so freaked out, aren't you ready to settle down? This should be a good thing. Cole is a great guy, he's gorgeous, successful and he likes you." I kept babbling to myself, until my cell phone illuminated my dark office. It was Cole, yet again. I pressed ignore and turned on my computer, if I was here I might as well start preparing my documents for my City Council hearing next week.

I was plugging away on my document preparation when the security guard knocked on my office door. I jumped in my chair, startled. "Hi, may I help you?"

"Yes, ma'am, there's a man in your lobby who says he's here to meet with you? I wasn't sure if he was telling the truth or not, as it is a little late for visitors, so I suggested I come up and check with you before sending him in."

"Did you get his name?"

"Yes, ma'am, Cole Conrad."

My heart jumped, why had he come all the way down here? He was supposed to be at dinner with his parents. "Thank you, please send him back." The security guard walked towards our lobby and within a few seconds Cole marched into my office.

He stood in the doorway for a moment looking around. "Are you okay? It seems pretty quiet here, must have been some emergency."

I looked down at my computer screen, not sure of what to say, then I stared back into his eyes. "Yes, I'm fine. We just had something come up and I needed to make sure it was squared away for a meeting with the council members."

He came in, sat across from me, and leaned back in his chair, cupping his hands behind his head. "So, whatever it was that you had to work on was so important that you couldn't even tell me you were leaving, you just walked out?" He looked out the window over the night cityscape, gathering his thoughts. Taking a deep breath, he said, "I'm sorry, Reagan, but I'm not buying it, what really happened?" His mother's words replayed in my head? How could I possibly tell him what she relayed to me? Instead I looked out the window, unsure as to what I would say. "Babe, come on, talk to me," he demanded in an irritated voice.

I stood up and started pacing back and forth behind my desk, cracking my knuckles out of pure mortification as I began to speak. "Okay, there wasn't an emergency, well, not here at the office, at least. Your mom and I were on the balcony talking and she was telling me all about your job and how successful you are and how you built the hotel and that her and your dad are so proud of you, but they know something is missing in your life and then she went on and on about how you have had a ton of women, but she's never seen you look at a woman the way you look at me and she was basically insinuating that we are perfect for each other and it freaked the shit out of me." I blurted out without stopping or pausing to take a breath. Before he could interrupt me I drew in a quick breath, and went right on explaining. "I had to get out of there before I had a panic attack. I mean, I know I like you, but I don't think I'm ready to think that far out, yet. And when she said it, I kind of just freaked and had to leave. I don't want to disappoint your parents by not being the woman they want me to be for you. I'm sorry, I panicked, but that's just my nature, the littlest things freak me out and I have to just get away and deal with them on my own. I know it's immature, but since my parent's death it's just how I deal with things, I panic." I leaned against the side of the desk, catching my breath after the rant I had just been on.

He sat in his chair looking at me. "Are you finished?"

I began pacing again, *I think so, but I'm not sure. Damn it. Why am I so screwed up when it comes to this man?* "For now."

"Good." He rose out of his seat, and walked over to me, picking me up off of the floor and setting me down on top of my desk, he slid between my legs. "First things first, I love my mother, but she's a meddler. I'm her only child and she doesn't understand how I am twenty-nine years old and still not settled down, yet. She assumes that because she and dad found each other at eighteen the rest of the world, including myself, has to do the same." He leaned in closer to my face, cupping my cheeks in his giant hands as he gently placed a kiss on my forehead. "And second off, she's right." I gasped for air, panic rising inside me, yet again. Cole ran his thumb over my bottom lip as he leaned back and let out a light laugh. Looking deep into my eyes he continued, "Calm down, we've really got to work on these panic attacks, when I say she's right I mean, yes, I do look at you differently than I did the other women I've been with. I've got to be perfectly honest here, when I woke up the morning after Addison's bachelorette party and you were gone I was hurt. For the first time in my life I'd hoped the woman I had gone to bed with was still there when I woke up. And when you weren't it was like I was finally getting a taste of my own medicine and I was pissed."

He stopped talking for a minute and sat in my chair, pulling himself up under the desk, so he was positioned between my legs, placing his firm grip on my hips. His dark eyes shot up to meet my gaze. "Reagan, I knew from the minute I looked into your eyes that you were different. You challenge me without even realizing it and I love that about you, who knows what the future holds for us, but for right now, I just want us to try and make this work."

"Make what work, Cole? It was a one night stand that led into a forced date by my best friend."

He leaned back running his fingers through his hair. "Damn, you're impossible. I'm telling you what I want and you're still avoiding it. Let me lay it out for you; you're an attorney so you are used to dealing with contracts, right?" I nodded, wondering where he was going with this. "Okay, so let's make this clear for you." He grabbed a legal pad off of my desk and reached for a pen, then began scribbling something onto the paper. I tried to peer over the pad and see what he was writing, but he kept moving it out of my view. Finally, he'd finished writing and handed me the legal pad. I took it from him and began reading what he had written.

Contract
Do you agree to be my girlfriend?
___ Yes
___ No

Reagan Larson (Signature)

"You need a refresher course in contracts!" I exclaimed, giggling like a school girl.

"Just answer the damn question, Reagan."

I took my favorite pen out of the side drawer of my desk, checked my answer, signed the signature block, handed it back to Cole, and watched as the most earth shattering smile ripped across his face. He was instantly on his feet, grasping my face between his hands, as his lips began to conquer mine.

Heat flushed over my entire body. I noticed the tingle that was quickly taking over deep in the pit of my stomach. Any man that could have my body go from zero to a million in a millisecond had to be a keeper. A loud moan escaped my throat as I dropped my head back. Cole instantly took the invitation to devour my neck, which was more than fine by me. Our breathing began to quicken. His hands were working their way under my dress, up my thighs. And in that very moment I was thanking myself for the earlier wardrobe fiasco, that black dress wouldn't have been as cooperative.

His teeth grazed over my shoulder, stilling his hands at the hem of my panties, his heavy breath bathing my neck. "Please tell me you have condoms here?" *Are you serious? Why would I have condoms in my office?*

"No. You don't have any in your wallet?"

He straightened up, pulling his wallet from his back pocket rifling through it. "Damn, nothing."

I leaned my forehead on his chest and let out a tiny

laugh. "Well, my dear, it looks like we are going to have to call it a night."

He kissed the top of my head rubbing my back. "I was afraid you were going to say that." He grabbed my hand, helping me off of the desk. We left my office and he drove me home.

Once we arrived at my house, he opened the car door, helping me out, leading me to the porch. I pulled my keys from my clutch and wiggled them into the lock, opening the door as Cole wrapped his arms around me, pulling me against his firm chest.

"I really don't want to say goodbye, any chance you're interested in overnight company?"

I slid my hands up his massive chest, wrapping them around his neck as I drew him to me and placed a soft kiss on his lips. "I'd love for you to stay over, but I have to be back in the office early tomorrow morning. We've got a huge zoning hearing coming up and I'm already far enough behind from the wedding, so I think I'm going to have to pass on this one."

He rolled his head back and took in a deep breath. "Fine, but I'm only leaving because I know I can come back anytime and no longer have to worry about you running out on me."

I dipped my head embarrassed and he pulled me tighter against his body. "I love those red cheeks, they're much better than a panic attack," he joked, leaning down plastering a kiss on my lips that tempted me to invite him in. "I better run before this gets out of hand." Kissing my lips one last time, he walked down the steps of my porch. Reaching his car, he turned over his shoulder and said, "Contracts, I never knew they could be so fun."

I laughed hollering back, "I hope you realize that one isn't legally binding!" I donned a cheesy grin as I watched him drive off, closing the door behind me.

Chapter Ten

Work was crazy busy the next two weeks as I had prepped for, attended, and won one of our biggest zoning hearings. Cole and I hardly had any time to talk, much less see each other, so I was looking forward to 4p.m. that Friday afternoon, very much. Cole was picking me up from work and he and I were going on a weekend getaway. My assistant knocked on my door before she burst in with the biggest smile I'd ever seen on her face. "Umm, so there is this guy in reception here to see you. I'm not sure who he is, but I'm pretty positive he could quite possibly be a supermodel."

I laughed, peering at my watch thinking he was fifteen minutes early. "Is he super tall, brown hair, tanned skin and a killer body?"

She fanned her face before sighing, "Oh yea, that's him."

"That would be the new boyfriend. Would you mind bringing him back?" I could tell by the way she squealed with excitement and clapped her hands that she didn't mind at all.

A few moments later Cole was walking into my office. "Hey, babe, you ready to go?" he asked, placing a kiss atop my head. He hovered over me for a brief minute, taking in the smell of my hair. "Damn, I've missed you."

"You're early, give me ten more minutes, and then we can head out." He sat down on the couch adjacent from my desk and pulled out his iPhone to check emails, I'm sure. Just then one of the senior partners walked past my office and stopped in the doorway.

"Colton Conrad, what brings you to Ms. Larson's office, is she helping you with a new development?"

Cole stood up and shook his hand. "Actually, I'm here to pick her up."

"Is that so?" he said, bewildered.

"Yes, sir, Reagan is my girlfriend and as soon as she finishes up, she and I are heading out of town for the weekend."

"Wonderful, will you be here a while, I have a few projects I'd like to throw your way?" Cole looked at me. I smiled at him, giving him the go ahead. "As much as I'd love to talk business, right now, I've spent the last two weeks away from this beautiful woman, so I'm going to have to respectfully decline, but I'll have my assistant set up lunch for the both of us next week."

"Sounds great, you two enjoy your trip. Keep her a few extra days if you'd like. That one right there is a hard worker, she could use more vacation time if you ask me." He said, winking towards me. I smiled at him and went back to finalizing my victory email to the junior associates who had worked so hard helping me secure our unanimous vote at the City Council hearing.

"Leave it up to you to know one of the most powerful attorneys in the state of Florida." I smiled as I typed away.

Cole strutted over to my desk and placed one hand on the back of my chair and the other on the desk next to me as he leaned in whispering into my ear, "If we're lucky we'll be able to mix business and pleasure." I flushed red and looked up into his eyes, filled with pure lust as he licked his lips. My body was instantly heating from the inside out, and I knew it was time to shut down the computer and get the hell out of the office. I fumbled with the mouse before Cole grabbed it and shut down the computer for me. Standing, Cole wrapped his arms around my hips, as I bent to grab my tote bag.

"Give me two seconds to change, I don't want to travel in these work clothes."

I began to walk out of my office as he muttered under his breath, "I agree, they aren't anywhere near as assessable as I'd like them to be." I grinned to myself and made my way to the bathroom, hailing my assistant to follow me in the process.

"How does this look?" I questioned my assistant, twirling in my new summer outfit.

"You look gorgeous. He's going to die."

I looked in the mirror and was pleased with what I saw. I may have been drowning in documents last week, but I was proud of my ability to still pull together a few cute outfits on my last minute shopping spree. I continued to study myself in the mirror. My long brown hair hung to the middle of my back in oversized loose curls and the teal color of my dress was bouncing off of my tanned skin. My legs looked phenomenal; the wedge sandals helped tremendously in extending their length. I put on a few pieces of jewelry to complete the outfit and grabbed my bag, heading towards the door.

"I'm so envious of you right now!" my assistant shouted, as I walked out of the restroom laughing. She had a great husband, but she was always living vicariously through my dating life, when I had one.

Cole was standing in the lobby, talking to another partner when I emerged. I caught his attention, he excused himself and reached for my hand, practically dragging me towards the elevators. "Can we please get the fuck out of here? I need to get under that dress." He whispered, forcing my body right up against his huge frame. The heat was rising again reminding me just how long it had been since he and I had more than thirty minutes together over the past two weeks. I began to breathe heavier than usual. Cole's fingers slid up the length of my arm, leaving a burning trail behind them. In that moment, I hoped wherever we were going wouldn't take long to get there.

The elevator chimed and before I could put one foot in front of the other Cole had me pressed against the wall of the elevator. His lips came crashing down upon mine in the fiercest kiss I'd had since meeting him. The tote bag dropped out of my hand, freeing my hands, so I clawed at his back, trying my best to pull his body even closer to mine. His right hand hooked my leg up around his hip, and he raised the hem of my dress up just enough over my thigh to expose my panties. He worked his hands up my legs, his tongue lashed my neck. Every inch of my body he touched turned to pure fire, and at the same time I could feel the pool of heat intensifying between my thighs.

Finally, his hand met the hottest part of my body. He slipped two fingers in, working my insides. My knee buckled beneath me. Cole pressed his entire weight onto my body, pinning me against the wall to keep me from toppling over. His fingers worked my insides, while his lips devoured every inch of my exposed chest. Moans ripped through my throat at the intense sensation building deep within me. *Damn this dress, why does it suddenly seem so restrictive? I need to get out of the damn thing.* I thought. Fortunately, I was jolted back to reality by the sound of the elevator doors beginning to open. Cole dropped my leg and adjusted my dress. Once I was presentable, he brought his two fingers to his mouth, sucking them clean. I gasped, trying to ensure my eyes didn't pop out of my head. "Fuck, baby, you taste as good as sin," he groaned, scooping my tote in one arm, and me in the other, guiding me out towards the SUV.

I melted against the passenger's seat with my eyes closed, trying to process my thoughts. *If he can push me almost completely over the edge in a thirty second elevator ride, just imagine the damage he could do when he finally has the time to focus on every inch of my body.* My entire body shuddered just thinking about it. A smile spread across my face at the same time I felt his hand reach for mine.

"What's going on in that brain of yours?" he probed, bringing my hand to his lips.

"I was just thinking about that elevator ride and how I wished it'd lasted longer." Cole gave me a reassuring smile and continued driving down the highway caressing my hand. "Where are we going anyways? I'm ready to get out of this car."

Cole laughed, looking down at the clock in the dash. "Another ten minutes and we'll be there, cool your jets, babe." I leaned over towards him and planted light kisses on his neck, working my hand under his shirt and over his muscled chest. My tongue began trailing over the five o'clock shadow along his jaw, my hand on its way down his chest towards his belt buckle. The second I began fidgeting with his buckle he reached across the SUV, unhooked my seatbelt, and in one swift move had me out of my seat and straddling his lap. I erupted in laughter, adjusting myself on his lap, ensuring he had a full view to the road.

"Can you see?" I asked.

"Yes, just get this fucking dress off, now!" He shouted in a deep throaty voice. *Oh, please, let that be black out tint on those windows.* I ripped my dress over my head and threw it in the passenger's seat as Cole motioned for me to lose the bra. And seconds later it accompanied the dress in a pile, where less than two minutes ago I'd been sitting.

His right hand clutched the steering wheel. His left arm wrapped tightly around my waist, pulling me closer to him, taking my breasts into his mouth as he teased my nipples with his teeth. He continued to tease me, causing my body heat to elevate all over again. My hands entwined in his hair pulling him closer. I began working my hips on his lap, feeling the bulge in his pants growing beneath me.

"Fuck, baby, I've got to concentrate on the road or I'm going to kill us both."

I leaned my head back, encouraging him to continue working my breasts. "What. A. Great. Way. To. Die." I said between breaths, thankful we'd actually made it to the secluded private road that led to the house. His body shook with laughter. I felt the vibrations all the way to my core. His left hand left my waist, working back around to my hips; before I knew it he was massaging the one spot sure to send me right over the edge. I panted for breath, pressing against his fingers harder.

"These have got to go, they're in the way," he said, plucking at my panties.

I tried my best to figure out a way to get them off without leaving his lap, but it was impossible. "I-I can't, I'll have to get off of you...just rip them off!" I begged, needing his skin on mine. The words barely flew out of my mouth before Cole had my panties torn off and thrown into the pile with the rest of my clothes. His fingers pressed deep inside of me as his thumb worked me over. Grasping his shoulders for leverage, my body rolled with every tweak of his fingers. "Cole!" I gasped, throwing my head back in pure gratification. I could feel his eyes peering into me while he watched what he was doing to my entire body.

"Come on, baby, I need to see you come. I've waited so long." His voice breathy and heated as he spoke and just like that, with his verbal command my body shook as sparks flew out of every nerve ending known to man. My nails dug into his shoulders as I rode out one of the greatest orgasms of my life, right there on his lap. Collapsing onto his shoulder, I tried to catch my breath. He continued driving, while tracing my bare back with his fingers, letting me have time to compose myself. Cole kissed the top of my head, "I'd say that's a good start to our long weekend, what do you think?"

I was still breathing heavily into his neck, but I tried to respond, "I...umm, yes, God yes....that was perfect." And with that I gave into my heavy eyelids and let exhaustion take over my body.

Chapter Eleven

I shuddered awake to the cool ocean breeze pricking my skin. Pulling the covers up to my chin, I realized we must have arrived while I was passed out on Cole's lap in the car. The moon was high in the sky and the stars were twinkling bright over the beautiful crashing waves of the ocean. I stretched my entire body, looking for Cole in the process, but all I saw was a giant bedroom. I sat up and noticed a white silk robe lying on the edge of the mattress. Crawling out of bed I covered my naked body and walked to the grand French doors, overlooking the white sandy beach.

I stood there taking it all in for a moment when I spotted Cole sitting across the way, lounging in a hammock working on his laptop. What a beautiful sight he was, lying there in nothing but a pair of running shorts. I slowly walked across the back patio towards him, taking my sweet time, since I enjoyed the view, all the while trying to not disturb his work. When I got closer he heard my steps and looked up from his computer, a smile spread across his face as he set his laptop down and motioned for me to come lie next to him. I climbed in next to him, snuggling right up to his warm body.

"How was your nap?"

"Much needed, I didn't realize how exhausted I'd been after the hearing." He kissed my forehead, and he rolled us both so he was on top of me, holding his body inches from mine.

"Good, because that's all the rest you are going to get." And with that his lips were on my neck, his fingers tracing their way down the edge of my robe, towards the bow holding it closed. Pulling my robe open, Cole began to shower my entire body with kisses. My skin was covered in goose bumps; I was beginning to realize this was just a natural reaction to his touch. As he worked his way down my chest and over my belly, I caught his face with both hands.

He looked up, trying to figure out why I had stopped him from going any further south. "What's wrong?"

I pulled him up to me, so we were face to face and kissed his lips. "I want to be in charge this time." You could see the excitement in his eyes as he leapt off of the hammock and pulled me into his arms. Wrapping my legs tightly around his waist, he carried me straight over to the couch in the gazebo. Setting me down he held me at arm's length, taking in the sight of my semi-naked body, still partially wrapped in the silk robe, being plastered to my curves by the gentle breeze.

After giving him a minute to enjoy the view, I slowly traced my fingers up over his chest. His hands rose to my hips, as I lifted myself up on my tiptoes to reach his neck with my lips. Slowly trailing my lips from one side of his neck to the other, his head rolled back and a moan escaped his throat. I looked up and smiled at him. I moved from his neck to his collarbone, then down his chest. I raked my teeth over his hard nipples, causing the rise and fall of his chest to become more rapid. His hands began moving over my breast. I grabbed them and placed them back on my hips. Looking up into his eyes, I twirled my tongue around his left nipple, reminding him that I was in charge and he was just here to enjoy himself.

I could tell he was getting anxious, so I began my descent down his abs, kissing every inch of his stomach until I was on my knees in front of him, trailing a path of light kisses on the skin right over his waistband. I took his hips into my hands and leaned back, taking in the bulge that was awaiting me under his shorts. I looked up into his eyes that were lit by the moonlight and begging me not to stop as he whispered, "Baby, please, don't stop." And at that command my hands grasped the hem of his shorts and ripped them down around his ankles. He sprang free and I took in the sight of the glorious man that was standing in front of me, beyond ready for whatever it was I was willing to give him. Smiling at his readiness, I licked my lips in anticipation of taking him fully into my mouth. I slowly slid his length in my mouth, adjusting to his size. He groaned, his hands going straight for my hair, grasping at it like it was his lifeline, while thrusting himself further into my mouth. *Damn, he tastes so good.* I thought to myself, feeling him growing larger with every pass of my tongue. He was thoroughly enjoying himself, as was I.

Peering up at him, I could see the pleasure racking his body as his chest rose up and down with his heavy breathing. He was beautiful and I loved the fact that I could get him worked up like that, but I wasn't ready to finish. Releasing him from my mouth, I slowly rose to my feet and sucked his earlobe into my mouth, whispering, "How was that?" into his ear.

His hands pulled me into his body, his erection pressed up against my belly. Catching his breath he leaned into my neck and in a breathy voice replied, "Fucking amazing."

I grinned and pushed him back onto the couch. Letting the robe fall from my shoulders, I climbed on top of his lap, straddling him and said, "Well, it's only going to get better." I reached for his shorts, finding exactly what I was looking for in the pocket. Smiling at the gold foil packet, I ground my wet readiness on his erection as I ripped it open with my teeth. "I see you came prepared this trip?" Cole smiled up at me, nodding in agreement. *Thank goodness.*

I quickly had the condom rolled down his entire length and I grabbed his shoulders for leverage. Lifting myself over his lap I slowly slid my body down on top of him. He filled me completely. I began thrusting my hips back and forth, slowly rotating them as Cole's mouth caressed every inch of my chest, teasing my nipples. His hands came up to guide my hips. My head flew back in such pleasure. I began to speed up. Cole meeting me thrust for thrust.

The sensation was paralyzing, my entire body was tingling with so much sensation I could hardly concentrate. My breath was faltering as I worked myself as fast as I could. Cole's hands gripping my ass while I worked us both over the edge. Exploding around him, I dug my nails into his shoulders. He quickly joined me in release, his fingers gripping my thighs as he came apart inside of me. His breath heavy against my chest, as he whispered, "Damn, babe, I could do that every hour of every day."

Laughing softly, I kissed his perfect lips. "Oh, trust me, so could I."

The next morning I wanted nothing more than to sleep in, since Cole and I had spent the majority of the evening doing anything other than sleeping, but that seemed to be impossible the third time my phone rang. Fumbling to find it on the nightstand, I answered it. "Hello," I said in a sleepy voice?

"Reagan!" I heard shouting from the other end. I sat straight up, so excited to hear the voice on the other end.

"Addison, are you home? What in the heck are you doing up so early on a weekend?" I questioned, getting out of bed, pulling my robe on as I made my way to the kitchen, trying not to wake Cole.

"Yes, Case and I got in last night. I'm still on Fiji time, sorry, I didn't mean to wake you, but now that you're up why don't you get dressed and come over? I'm dying to see my best friend."

My heart began to speed up, realizing I'd hardly talked to Addison her entire honeymoon, and she had no idea how deep I was in with Cole. "I umm... well, I..." I nervously laughed into the phone.

"What is it, spit it out?" she barked.

"Well, I sort of can't come over right now."

"And why in the hell not?"

"Well, I'm out of town... well, not out of town, out of town, just over at the beach out of town."

"Are you at the condo?" Addison's parents had a penthouse condo on Pass-a-Grille beach that we always went to for relaxing weekends.

"Not exactly, I'm a little further south, Anna Maria Island. I'm just here for the weekend, it's been crazy at work."

"Perfect, Case and I'll drive down and spend the day with you, I've missed you so much, and I can't wait any longer to tell you all about the honeymoon."

I chuckled as I reached for the orange juice in the refrigerator. "Umm, you may want to hold off on driving down, I'm not exactly by myself."

She gasped into the phone and the next thing I heard was Addison yelling across the house to Case. "OMG babe, Reagan and Cole are at the beach house on Anna Maria Island, together!" I laughed at her excitement as she put the phone back up to her ear. "Reagan, you have to tell me everything. I need to get caught up, I feel like I've missed so much while we were away."

"Oh you definitely have," at that I heard a throat clear. I whipped around to see Cole standing in the doorway of the kitchen, leaning against the doorframe in nothing but a pair of low hanging sweats. "Umm, Addison, I have to get going, can I call you later?"

She squealed into the phone like a child, "Call me as soon as you get home!"

"Ok, love you, bye." Hanging up the phone.

Cole walked over to me and kissed my lips, he tasted like mint from his toothpaste. "Good morning" he said, wrapping me into his arms.

"Mornin', sleep well?"

"Never better," he replied with a smile, as he pulled out a barstool and sat down. "How are the newlyweds?"

Smiling, I poured him a glass of orange juice. "Blissfully happy, they just got home last night, so they're still on Fiji time. Of course, Addison wanted me to come over. When I told her I was at the beach, she insisted on coming out to see me and that's when I had to break the news that I wasn't alone."

Cole laughed and ran his fingers through his tousled hair. *Damn, he looked so good when he did that.* "Do you want them to come out, so you can see her today?"

I set my glass on the counter in front of me and tilted my head to the side, looking at him with a 'you've got to be kidding me' expression.

"As much as I love my best friend, I think I can handle a few more days away from her, besides, I intended on being with you only, this weekend." I walked around, scooted between his legs, and planted a swift kiss on his lips.

"Good," he said, "now go get dressed. We have somewhere to be in fifteen minutes.

I turned and headed in the direction of the bedroom. I put on the new bikini from Addison and I modeled it in the mirror. "Shit, this wasn't a good idea. This thing practically crawls up my entire ass," I said to myself as I looked over my shoulder at my butt in the mirror.

"I think it looks perfect," Cole said, walking into the room in a pair of board shorts, a fishing shirt, and flip flops. "And as much as I'd love to see you prancing around in that all day, I think you're going to have to put something over it, or I may have to fight off the guys on the boat."

"Boat" I asked, sounding confused.

"Yes, I rented us a charter so we could go fishing today, I hope you don't mind?" *Fishing! Oh yes, he was perfect.* I may be a total girly girl, but my dad raised me right. He taught me to love the finer things in life, while also enjoying the outdoors and all that came with them.

We spent the entire day out on the water catching fish after fish, it was perfect. And that evening Cole made me relax by the pool while he prepared some of the grouper we caught earlier that day. It was just perfect, the sun was setting over the ocean, the sky was painted in pinks and purples, like something you would see in a gallery, and Cole was manning the grill, while I sipped my wine relaxing in a chaise lounge at the pools edge. The fish smelled delicious, along with the vegetables he was grilling up to go with dinner. Before he finished up I'd grabbed the plates and utensils, and set the patio table, so we could eat outside. Dinner was beyond my expectations. Cole was a phenomenal cook, and the dessert, homemade key lime pie, he'd prepared was even better. We took the pie down to the edge of the water and sat down on a blanket as we ate dessert.

"What were your parents like?" I looked at Cole, caught off guard, surprised by his question that had come out of nowhere. I loved my parents, but I didn't like to talk about them, it made me too emotional. I looked away from Cole's eyes, pulling my knees to my chest, hoping he'd change the subject. He scooted closer to me and wrapped his arm around my waist. "Babe, please tell me about them. I feel like I'd know you better if I knew about your parents."

I felt my eyes well up with tears, as I turned back to him. "They were wonderful, Cole." I smiled at the memories I had of both my mother and father. They were the best memories of my life.

"What was it like growing up with them?"

I closed my eyes and laid back on the blanket,

remembering. "It was like a fairytale, literally. My parents were so in love. I've never seen two people that infatuated with one another. And it wasn't that annoying make you want to vomit love; it was true love, once in a lifetime love. You looked at them and you were jealous of what they shared, because you knew nothing would ever compare." I took a few deep breaths, trying to keep my emotions in check. I felt Cole lean in and kiss a tear away from my cheek.

"Their relationship was everything I ever hoped for when I grew up. It was never about one or the other, rather the two of them as a whole, and then when I came along it was about the three of us. We were all inseparable."

"Well, if you are any indication of the people they were, then I truly wish I could've met them." I smiled up at him as he kissed my lips.

"Do you think they would have liked me?"

I propped myself up on my elbows and smiled at his question, wondering what my parents would have thought about Cole. "As long as they could see that you truly cared about me, they both would have loved you."

He sat up and I just laid there, both of us silent for a few moments. "You know I care about you, right?" he asked.

I sat up next to him. "Of course, I do."

He smiled, then turned and faced me, grabbing my hands. "I really care about you, Reagan. I've had a connection with you from the minute I met you and I know it's only been a little over a month, but I'm falling in love with you, no, not falling, have already fallen in love with you. I love you, Reagan Larson."

I stared up at him, eyes as big as the moon, replaying the words, "I love you," over and over again in my head. I'd waited so long to hear these words from someone, who I could really see my future with, and now that it was happening I could hardly believe it.

After what seemed like an eternity, Cole grasped my

shoulders and pulled me out of my trance. "Breathe, Reagan."
I looked up into his eyes, remembering to breathe. "It's ok if
you don't say it back. I just needed to tell you how I felt about
you."

I got up on my knees, so I was face to face with him, put
my hands on his cheeks, placed my forehead on his, closing
my eyes for a moment, and took a deep breath. "Colton
Conrad, you have no idea how long I have waited to hear
those words. I never imagined I could love anyone like my
parents loved each other, until I met you. We may have had a
bumpy beginning, but there is no one else I could imagine
myself with, I love you so, so much." And at my response his
mouth took over mine and as the world around us
disappeared, Cole and I made sweet, sweet love under the
stars to the sounds of the crashing waves.

Chapter Twelve

After spending four wonderful days at the beach house with Cole, it was time to get back to reality, and reality meant work. Cole had a business trip to Phoenix and I had to get caught up, it seemed ever since I had met him all I was doing was trying to catch up at the office. Luckily, my assistant had been a huge help, allowing me to leave early on Wednesday for my dinner date with Addison. She'd been back a few days and was going crazy over the fact that we'd yet to see each other, so that afternoon I met her for drinks and dinner.

"My oh my, you totally have that I've been doing it for days smile on your face right now!" She exclaimed as I walked across the restaurant towards her seat at the bar. The two men sitting next to her quickly glanced over at me and looked me up and down, smiling like they could possibly be next.

My cheeks flushed and I hugged my best friend while cursing her to hell in my head. "Could you be any louder?"

She snickered and said, "Well, I'm sorry, could you be any more obvious?" We both laughed, and I ordered a drink from the bartender.

"So, tell me all about your honeymoon. I'm dying to hear

ONE NIGHT WITH HIM

about Fiji, you know that's on my list of places to visit before I'm thirty."

Addison glared at me while taking a sip of her Chardonnay. "If you think I came here to talk about my honeymoon you must be out of your mind, you know me so much better than that, Reagan Larson, now spill it, I want every detail. When I left you practically wanted to rip Cole's balls off and serve them up on a silver platter, and now it's all flowers and rainbows, this story has got to be good." I blushed again and knew it was better I just give in and get it over with. Three hours later Addison and I sat in the corner booth of the restaurant and she was just looking at me completely stunned. "Well my dear, I do believe you have managed to do the impossible."

I looked at Addison confused. "And what's that?" I asked.

"You've managed to bring Cole Conrad to his knees."

"Oh, stop it, Addison. I'm not the first girl he's ever fallen in love with, I'm just probably the only one you've ever liked."

"Only one any of us have ever liked, trust me, I'm family now, and word on the street is everyone loves you and Cole together. They've all been rooting for you since they saw the connection the two of you had at the wedding. And as for falling in love, Cole doesn't fall in love, so I'd say you're wrong, you're the first girl he's ever fallen for."

I quickly pulled my glass of wine to my lips sucking it down as I thought to myself, *Oh man, I'm in way too deep.*

On the drive home I couldn't stop thinking about what Addison said about Cole, I knew he lived the bachelor lifestyle, but surely he'd fallen in love before me, he was almost thirty years old for God's sakes. Phoenix was three hours behind us and I knew Cole was probably at a business dinner, but I wanted to text him to let him know I'd made it home safe and was getting ready for bed.

GOING TO BED, HOPE YOUR TRIP IS GOING WELL. CALL ME SOMETIME TOMORROW.

YOU OK? I MISS YOU.

YES, FINE, JUST TIRED. MISS YOU TOO.

YOU SURE?

I hesitated before responding, *I'm fine, but thanks to Addison all I wanted to know is if I was the only girl he's ever loved.* And at that thought, before I could even contemplate what I was texting I went on one of my typical Reagan rants.

I'M NOT SURE WHY THIS EVEN MATTERS, BUT I JUST HAVE TO KNOW IF ADDISON IS RIGHT. AM I THE ONLY GIRL YOU HAVE EVER FALLEN IN LOVE WITH? I KNOW YOUR PAST RELATIONSHIPS ARE NONE OF MY BUSINESS, BUT I'M JUST CURIOUS.

Did you really just ask him that, you've officially lost it? Snatching my phone back up, I began typing as quickly as my fingers would allow.

YOU KNOW WHAT, NEVERMIND, I'M SORRY I EVEN ASKED THAT, YOU'RE AT WORK AND YOU'RE BUSY. JUST FORGET ALL OF THIS. I'LL TALK TO YOU TOMORROW. GOODNIGHT COLE.

I set my phone down on the night stand, berating myself for pushing send on that stupid text. Drawing my covers up to my neck, I tried to force myself asleep. A few minutes later my phone started ringing. Cole's face was flashing on the screen. *Crap!* "Hello."
"Yes."

"Yes, what?"

"Yes, you're the only woman I've ever fallen in love with." My heart started pounding like a loud base drum, and the butterflies in my stomach were fluttering out of control. The smile that took over my face was quite possibly the biggest smile I'd ever had in my entire life and a sigh of relief escaped my throat. "Baby, I've got to get back to this dinner, but I just wanted to make sure you know it's you and only you."

A happy tear rolled down my cheek and I whispered into the phone, "I love you, Cole."

"I love you, too. Now get some rest and I'll call you in the morning, night babe."

Work was chaotic the next morning when Cole called, so I had to let it go to voicemail. We had just landed a huge project, and the partners wanted me to sit in on the first meeting. I was curious as to what we would be working on, with this group of guys you never knew what you were going to get, but it was always exciting. As the assistant passed around the portfolios the first thing I noticed was Cole's logo on the building drawing, and I smiled inwardly to myself, *oh yes, we were finally going to get to mix business and pleasure.*

One of the partners took the floor and began telling us all about our relationship with Conrad Developers, he'd obviously worked with them in the past and spoke very highly of Cole's company. Going over everyone's role in the project I was named supervising attorney, which meant I would be in charge of all of the associates working on the development, overseeing all of the legal aspects of the entire project. The meeting was short and I was thrilled to begin working with Cole.

Just as I was gathering my things, one of the partners grabbed me and pulled me aside, "Ms. Larson, I want to let you know we are very excited about our partnership with Conrad Developers. Your management of this project is a great opportunity for your shot at becoming our youngest partner in the firm."

My stomach flipped at hearing the words roll off of his tongue. I'd dreamt of becoming partner, but I'd never imagined I'd potentially make it there before thirty. "Thank you, sir, it's such a privilege to be able to work on this project. I'm truly grateful for the opportunity."

Driving to the airport to pick up Cole that afternoon, I was still reeling from my meeting with the partners, and wondering if he knew they picked me to be the supervising attorney. As I pulled into the arrivals bay, he stood under the Delta sign completely oblivious to the handsomeness that was radiating off of him, his hair blowing slightly in the breeze, and his tie hanging loosely from his neck.

He caught a glimpse of my car and looked straight up into my eyes. The magnitude of the smile that spread over his face sent chills down my spine. I pulled up next to him, and before I knew it his bags were in the backseat, he'd jumped into the passenger's side and taken my face between his palms, his lips softly pressed against mine. He showered me in quick light kisses before looking deep into my eyes, placing his forehead on mine, he let out a sigh and whispered, "I missed you so much."

I giggled as I pulled away and grabbed his hand. "It's only been a few days, you couldn't have missed me that much." He leaned back in the seat and closed his eyes. "You tired?" He grunted, and I took that as a yes. "I have some good news, well its good news to me, hopefully you'll feel the same." Cole opened those golden eyes and stared over at me, waiting in anticipation. "I was pulled into a meeting this morning and named supervising attorney on the Imperial Park Condo project, looks like you and I are going to be spending a lot more time together." His eyes lit up as a grin took over his face. "And better yet, assuming everything goes according to plan on this project, it'll set me up for partnership with the firm."

Cole kissed my hand, and looked genuinely happy with the news. "Babe, that's incredible. I'm so happy for you. I know partnership is definitely what you want. Are you excited?"

Of course, I was excited, I was beyond excited. I was twenty-seven and already being considered for partner, this was one of my biggest dreams. "Yes! I'm thrilled. But I'm trying not to get ahead of myself, we still have to see how the project goes, one mistake and it could be over."

He glanced at me like I was insane. "Not going to happen, you're one of the best attorney's I've ever met. They'd be crazy not to make you partner." I smiled as I drove to Cole's, ecstatic with his reaction.

Chapter Thirteen

Three tedious months passed while I worked on contract after contract with my team of associates. I knew my career depended on this project, so I immersed myself in my work, only taking the weekends off to rest. Luckily for Cole and me we saw each other almost every day, since we worked hand in hand during the entire process. And it had been completely worth it, not only had the development moved faster than anticipated, which was great for the firm, but Cole and I had grown so much closer as a couple it was amazing.

Tonight we were at the hotel getting ready for the cocktail party Cole's company was hosting in honor of the groundbreaking that had taken place earlier that morning. Cole was downstairs picking up his suit from the cleaning staff, and I was in his large bathroom getting dolled up by a hair and makeup artist Addison had hired for me as a congratulatory gift. She was thrilled this part of the project was over; it meant that she and I could get back to spending more quality time together. She constantly joked with Cole that Conrad Developers had selfishly stolen her best friend away from her in the interest of the owner of the company.

"What do you think?" The beautician asked as she spun me around in the chair to look in the mirror.

I gasped when I saw myself. No wonder Addison always used this girl, she's brilliant. I thought as I examined my hair and make-up in the giant mirror. My dark brown hair was perfectly curled and pinned loosely to the side, so it flowed down my shoulder and my make-up was bold, but still simple enough to look elegant. It was a spot on match with the emerald green cocktail dress I was getting ready to slip into. "Thank you so much, I look amazing, and I don't even have my dress on yet." We both laughed as she gathered her things and I walked her to the door.

When Cole returned from picking up his suit, I was dressed and having a glass of wine on the balcony with Addison and Casey, who were coming along as our guests to the party. After getting dressed, Cole joined us on the balcony and proposed a toast, "To spending an incredible evening with my best friend, his beautiful wife, and the love of my life." We all clinked glasses and drank to that. Cole slipped his arm slowly around my waist and pulled me closer to him as he whispered into my ear, "You look absolutely stunning," kissing my neck, I giggled as he finished his sentence, "and I cannot wait to get you out of that dress later on." I instantly felt my body heat and send shivers right down to the pit of my belly.

I looked up into his eyes as I wrapped my free hand around his tie, pulling him closer to my face, resting my forehead on his. "What's under this dress is all yours, baby." And with the devilish grin he gave me I could no longer contain myself, even knowing we had an audience. I used his tie to pull him closer and plastered my lips to his, reaching directly for his hair, tangling my fingers in it as his arm pulled me tighter against his rock hard body. His tongue dove into my mouth, the taste of wine still lingered in his mouth. I could feel his erection beginning to form behind his pants and knowing my kiss alone turned him on spiked my arousal even more. I pressed harder into him, knowing it was physically impossible to be any closer than I was, when a throat cleared behind us.

"Umm, guys, as happy as we are that the two of you are so in love, we'd rather get to this party than watch the two of you seduce each other on the balcony." We slowly pulled apart from each other. I turned in Cole's arms and gave an apologetic smile to Casey. Of course, Addison was watching like she was at a damn Hollywood movie premiere.

"Freak," I mouthed at her laughing.

"Skank," she mouthed back.

And on that note, the guys decided it was time to head to the party. Cole held the door to the elevator, as we all stepped out into the rooftop lounge of the hotel. The band played light jazz music in the background and the breeze whipped around us, the smell of the saltwater lingering behind it. There wasn't a cloud in the sky, and from the looks of it the party would be labeled quite a success. Cole placed my arm through his, then we headed towards the crowd to say hello.

We spent the next hour mingling with different people from my firm, Cole's company, and, of course, our guest. Everything was going perfectly. Cole's assistant Heather had done a fabulous job of making sure the evening was just right. Just as we'd all made our way back to each other, the cocktail waitress passed and we each took a glass of champagne.

"How's the champagne?" Heather asked, coming up from behind the four of us.

"It's wonderful, thank you, Heather." Cole responded.

"Glad to hear that, I was sure to get your favorite, Mr. Conrad." She said, winking at him. Addison of course shot a 'what the fuck' look in my direction.

I just rolled my eyes at her. "Heather, you look wonderful, this event is great. You did such a fine job preparing everything and making sure it all came together perfectly."

"Of course, Mr. Conrad expects nothing but perfection, and that's exactly what I give him." There was Addison again with the look.

I just smiled as Cole reached over, drew me closer to him, and placed a kiss atop of my head.

"Would you all excuse us, please, we need to freshen up." Addison said, grabbing my arm and hauling me towards the ladies room. She stormed into the restroom and locked the door behind us. I went towards the mirror to apply another coat of lipstick and Addison was at my side in an instant. "There's something about that little bitch that I don't like."

I laughed in the mirror. "Addison, calm down. Heather is a very nice girl, she's been working for Cole for five years or something like that. She's just trying to make sure everything is perfect for him."

"Exactly, everything including her tight little ass in that black hooker dress."

I pressed my hip up against the counter and glared into her eyes. I crossed my arms against my chest. "Look, I trust Cole, I know he was the white Rico Suave before I came along, but he loves me and I know he'd never do anything with anyone, and that includes Heather. I can't get my panties in a wad every time some woman throws herself at him, it comes with the territory. As long as he respects me, I have no reason not to trust him."

She crossed her arms and stared back at me before relaxing. "Fine, just be careful. I know he loves you, and he'd never intentionally hurt you, but trust me, there are a million women out there who would be willing to make him try, including his trashy little assistant, Heather."

I hugged Addison. "Thank you, I'm so glad you're always looking out for me, but that man," I held her at arm's length, "has all the woman he could ever want right here." I laughed as I shook my body in a seductive motion, running my hands down the sides of my fitted dress over my hips. We both burst out laughing as she took my hand and we headed back to the party.

Cole and Casey were at the bar sipping their drinks, talking to some of the partners when Addison and I emerged from the ladies room. We decided against joining them, we'd had enough business talk for one evening. So we sat down at one of the lounge tables to people watch while sipping champagne. We must have sat there for an hour as Cole and Casey remained at the bar with a steady flow of patrons. All the while Addison and I were being bombarded by the wives of all of the attorneys. Most were interested in how Cole and I met, and some even asked about Casey, not knowing his wife was sitting right next to me. Addison would chime in every time, "Oh you mean my handsome husband?" And the women would quickly move along, terrified at what might come next.

"As much as I've enjoyed this party, I think Casey and I need to get going. It's getting late, and we have to be up early in the morning tomorrow, it's our Saturday morning ten mile run along Bayshore."

I looked at her, creasing my eyebrows together. "It's 11 p.m., you're bailing because you have to go for a run in the morning, what in the heck happened to my best friend?"

She laughed and pulled me up from my seat. "Come on, besides, don't you want to get back to what you and Cole started?" A flashback of being on the balcony replayed in my head and a smile spread across my face. *She does have a point.*

When we got to the bar Casey was finishing up his drink. "Where's Cole?" I asked looking around the room.

"There was some kind of issue in the kitchen and he went down to check it out. He left about fifteen minutes ago, I figured he'd be back by now." We stood at the bar for another five minutes, waiting for him to come back, but he didn't.

"I'm going to run downstairs and look for him, make sure

everything is okay." I left Casey and Addison, and hopped in the elevator. When the elevator reached the lobby, I stepped out onto the marble floor just as the doors across from me were preparing to close and inside I saw Cole's huge frame pressed up against the wall with a tiny body I instantly recognized -Heather- plastered on top of him, his hands gripping her waist as their lips crashed down upon one another.

Chapter Fourteen

The elevator doors closed in slow motion as Cole looked up from his kiss straight into my eyes. I stumbled backwards against the wall, as if a ton of bricks had just hit my chest knocking all of the wind out of my body. I couldn't breathe and I instantly felt a panic attack coming on. *Hold it together, Reagan, there are people from your office here tonight, don't lose it, not yet, just get to the car.*

I forced one foot in front of the other, and before I knew it I was running through the lobby towards the valet attendant. I threw my pass at the young man I'd come to know over the past few months and braced my knees, trying to keep myself from toppling over. My breath was so rapid I was terrified I'd hyperventilate right there.

"Ms. Larson is everything okay?" he asked.

In between breaths I choked out as many words as my body would allow. "Yes.Car.Please." I said, trying to catch my breath between each word.

He walked over towards me and placed a hand on my shoulder. "Are you sure you should be driving?"

"Just.Hurry." I choked out, holding back the sobs that

were ripping through my chest.

He was back in no time, and I was so grateful, before I could fully stand back up he was at my side, pulling me close to him as he helped me into my SUV. Closing my door behind me, I hit the gas and flew out of the parking lot. I had to get as far away from that hotel as physically possible, so I jumped on the interstate and just drove as fast as I could. I continued fighting the tears, knowing the minute I even let one escape it would be over, and I'd be too distraught to even drive. I turned the air conditioner on full blast, and pointed it straight at my face in the hopes that it would hold the tears back, and potentially help me calm my rapid breathing before I passed out. After twenty minutes of driving I'd finally arrived at exactly where I thought I needed to be. I threw my car in park, flung the door open, and collapsed on the patch of grass in front of me.

Catching myself, before my face smacked the ground, a sob escaped my throat and that was it, the tears pierced my eyelids and quickly began spilling over them as if someone had just turned the water faucet on full blast. Resting on my knees, I draped my arms around my stomach, when I lurched over holding myself as tight as possible, trying to keep from convulsing. But it was too hard, the sobs were so deep I was trembling from head to toe. My body ached like it's never ached before. Within a matter of thirty minutes I had gone from feeling completely on top of the world to feeling as if I had been hit time and time again by a semi-truck. Trying to compose myself, I leaned back against the tree that was to my right. I rested my head, and through my tear filled eyes, I came face to face with their headstone.

In Loving Memory of Sophia and Christopher Larson, Beloved Mother and Father. *Bad idea, Reagan!* In my head I'd thought it would've been a good idea to be this close to my mom and dad given my current state, but upon seeing their headstone I quickly realized it was the complete opposite.

Grabbing for the tree I pulled myself up off the ground, trying to balance myself as my stilettos sunk into the lush green grass.

"How could you both leave me?" I shrieked at their headstone. Tears pouring even harder, now that I'd added my parents into the mix of things. I stood there for a minute, actually thinking I may have gotten a response. "Why? I needed you both and you just left me, no warning, just gone!" I continued shouting through sobs. "Was I not good enough, did I not deserve either of you? Do I not deserve Cole? What is wrong with me, why does everyone I love get taken away?" My body was thoroughly exhausted as I fell back down to my knees. Sobbing, I leaned against their headstone and wrapped my arms around my body. I sat there crying, all alone, in the dark.

Several hours later, I awoke to what I thought was rain hitting my face. I jumped at the realization of where I had fallen asleep, looked around to see that the sun was coming up over the horizon, and that it wasn't rain, rather the sprinklers had turned on in the cemetery. I quickly stood up and looked down at my parent's grave. Resting my hand atop of it, I apologized for berating them the night before, "I'm so sorry, Mom, Dad. I just miss you both so much, there are so many things happening right now and I just wish the two of you were here to help me through all of them." I kissed my hand and placed it on each of their names, figuring I'd better get out of the cemetery before someone called the cops on the crazy lady who'd yelled at a headstone all night.

Climbing into my SUV the clock read 5:45 a.m. I pulled down my mirror and wasn't shocked at the amount of mascara that had stained my cheeks. That and the constant ache in my chest were sure fire reminders that last night actually happened. I reached for my phone and saw all of the missed calls; twenty-three from Cole, twelve from Addison, five from Casey, and two each from Addison's parents. I also had a full voicemail box. I wasn't in the mood to listen to any of them, so I just deleted everything with one press of a button, turned my phone off, and started my car.

Driving down my street I saw Cole's car parked in front of my house. I was half tempted to keep driving, but the crick in my neck and my wet clothes reminded that I needed to get cleaned up, and at least try to get a few more hours of sleep before the weekend was over. Pulling into the driveway I placed the car in park, reached for my clutch, and took a deep breath before I headed to my front door.

Cole was sitting on my porch swing passed out, obviously, having spent the entire night there awaiting my return. I tried my damnedest not to wake him, but when my key slid into the door his eyes flew open and he jumped off of the swing. "Where have you been? I've been waiting all night for you." I couldn't even look at him; I just pushed my door open and stepped in. His hand flew straight out catching the door before I could close it on him. "Reagan, please, we need to talk," he declared, panic in his voice.

I turned around to get one last glimpse of his beautiful face, and also hoping he would feel the same excruciating pain that I felt the night before when he looked into my eyes. "I'm done, Cole, I can't compete with those other women." The tears slowly started trickling down my cheeks and he sucked in a sharp breath at the sight of them.

Moving closer, shaking his head he looked up at me again. "Please, baby, don't say that, just let me explain." His hands reached out for mine and I pulled back from him before he could touch me.

"Cole, just go, please." I pushed the door closed behind me and locked it, as Cole beat on the wood from the outside.

"Damn it, Reagan, please just talk to me. You don't understand, please!" he shouted. I couldn't handle hearing his voice, so I ran to the shower, turned the hot water on, and cranked my iPod all the way up until it finally drowned out the sounds of fists banging on wood and shouting from my front porch. I leaned against the tile as the scalding water burned my skin, praying the pain of the hot water would eventually take over the pain I felt in my chest.

Chapter Fifteen

Emerging from the shower, I ran straight to my room, put on my most comfortable pajamas, set my iPhone on the music doc, hit repeat on my go to break up song, Brandy's *Have You Ever*, and climbed into bed, forcing myself to close my eyes and try my best to fall asleep. At least if I was sleeping I wouldn't feel the constant ache that had a hold of my entire body. As the lyrics played lightly over the speakers the tears began rolling down my face, again. I'd cried to this song after every break up since I was twelve years old, but this time it had an entirely different meaning. I'd never loved any of those guys, not the way I loved Cole. This time her words pierced my soul, shredding every ounce of hope I'd possibly had left.

"Reagan, wake up." My body shook as I felt light kisses trailing their way up my arm. I rolled over in bed and was staring into Cole's beautiful golden eyes. He leaned down and kissed my lips. "Wake up, we need to talk." I sat up wondering how he'd gotten into my house. "Look, Reagan, I love you, and these past six months have been wonderful, but there's something you need to know," he took a deep breath before finishing his sentence. "Heather and I have been together for the past three months and I just... I just feel a stronger

connection with her than I do with you."

The tears pricked my eyes and suddenly I heard a high pitched voice coming from my hallway, "Have you told her yet, sweetie?" Heather walked into my bedroom and my mouth fell open.

"GET OUT!" I screamed, pushing him off of my bed. "Get the hell out of my house, both of you!!!" How dare he bring her into my house. Heather looked over her shoulder as she took Cole's hand and pulled him out of my bedroom. "Told you I was perfect for him," she winked at me as they disappeared down the hall.

Flying off of the pillow, I sat up panting and looking around my bedroom, it was pitch black. I'd been asleep the entire day. Leaning back against my headboard, I'd realized that Cole and Heather being in my house had only been a dream. *Thank goodness*, I thought as I caught my breath. Looking at the clock I realized that I had slept all day and well into the next morning, it was 4 a.m. and I still felt exhausted. I climbed out of bed, grabbing my phone on my way into the kitchen to get a glass of water. I had more missed calls and numerous text messages. I deleted everything from Cole without reading or listening to them, only checking what was remaining from Addison.

YOU OK? PLEASE CALL ME.

REAGAN, PLEASE!

I'VE CALLED A MILLION TIMES, PLEASE JUST ANSWER ME.

I'M HERE, YOU MUST BE SLEEPING. CASE WON'T LET ME USE MY KEY. HE SAID I NEED TO LET YOU REST. I'M READY TO KILL HIM!

YOU UP YET? COLE KEEPS CALLING ME, I WON'T ANSWER.

REAGAN, HE'S HERE... HIM AND CASE ARE GOING FOR DRINKS.

HE LOOKS TERRIBLE. HE'S STILL IN HIS SUIT FROM LAST NIGHT.

I HATE HIM YOU KNOW. AS LONG AS YOU HATE HIM, I HATE HIM.

I KNOW YOU NEED YOUR ALONE TIME. I'LL TRY AGAIN TOMORROW. LOVE YOU REAGAN. I'M HERE WHENEVER YOU'RE READY.

I reached into the fridge and pulled out a bottle of water, lifting it to my lips as I walked back towards my bedroom. Passing the mirror in my dining room, I stopped to take a look at myself. My face was swollen and my eyes were a brutal combination of puffy and bloodshot. I looked like I hadn't slept in days. My hair was in a messy bun atop of my head and my body sagged in defeat. I was spent and felt like I could fall asleep right on my dining room table just from the tiny bit of walking I'd just done. I couldn't even make it back to my bedroom, the living room was closer, so I drug myself over to the couch and collapsed on top of it, falling asleep before I even hit the pillow.

Sunday was no different, I slept all day and when I awoke sometime in the middle of the night I decided I'd better let my office know I wasn't coming into work the next day. I pulled out my phone and sent my assistant an email.

To: dhammond@cmtlaw.com
From: rlarson@cmtlaw.com
Monday 2:33:07 AM
Subject: Out of Office

I won't be in the office today. I think I'm coming down with the

flu. I'll keep you posted. Tell Graham he is in charge of Imperial Park while I am out. I'm trying to get as much rest as possible, so please only contact me if it's an emergency.
-RL

I pressed send and fell right back asleep. That day I finally woke up around noon and for the first time in three days I actually didn't feel entirely exhausted, my stomach growling as I stretched in the afternoon sunlight shining through my window. I climbed off of the couch and went to the kitchen, pressing the Pandora app on my iPad, I began pulling everything I could find out of the refrigerator. I opened the windows and let the cool November breeze fill the kitchen, while I started prepping my stove. Sleeping for almost three days straight had left me starving. Half hour later I had a plate full of eggs, sausage, a toasted bagel and cream cheese, and a big bowl of fresh fruit. I'd decided that my eyes were bigger than my stomach, but I was determined to get out of my funk. A funk was fine when it was affecting my weekend, but now that it was affecting my work it was unacceptable.

I ate my breakfast, or lunch at that hour, and decided it was time to buck up. Of course, I was still hurting, in fact my heart hadn't ached this hard since my parents had passed, but I wasn't sixteen now, I'm twenty-seven years old and I have responsibilities, my career was at stake. I needed to forget about Cole and focus on my work. I decided I would spend the rest of the day pampering myself, and tomorrow I would get up and get my shit together. After I cleaned up my mess I picked up the phone to text Addison.

I'M ALIVE AND I NEED A MASSAGE. YOU FREE FOR A SPA AFTERNOON?

Not even thirty seconds later my phone was vibrating.

GET DRESSED, I'M ON MY WAY!!!

I ran to my room, knowing it would only take her five minutes to get to my house and threw on my favorite red maxi dress and a denim jacket. Looking in the mirror at myself, I decided after we had our massage hair and make-up would be next, then a manicure and pedicure, and then we'd go for dinner and drinks. Shortly after I pulled my sandals on, I heard Addison's horn honk. I grabbed my purse, walked outside, and hopped into the passenger's seat of her car. She leaned over and hugged me so tight.

"You okay?"

I squeezed her tight to reassure her of my answer, "never better." She gave me a worried smile and drove off, knowing that once I put something behind me it was easier to just leave it alone. My mom always told me the best thing about a mess was that it could always be cleaned up, and right now, we were on our way to clean up the mess I had made of myself over the past three days. Once that was done, I'd forget about it and move on.

The spa day had been just what the doctor ordered. The masseuse had worked all the tension out of my entire body, my hair and make-up look phenomenal, and I'd chosen a dark midnight purple for my mani/pedi.

"So where should we go for drinks?" Addison asked.

"Ocean Prime?" I suggested and her face lit up. They had a killer cocktail menu and the eye candy was always worth it.

"But first, we need something to wear," she said, waving her American Express Black card in the air. I smiled as she headed towards the mall.

Both dressed in skinny jeans and oversized knit sweaters, Addison zipped up her black boots, and I pulled my new brown knee high riding boots up my calves. We both posed in the mirror and I whispered, "Tory Burch, we wear you well." as Addison snapped a picture of the two of us.

The hostess seated us at our usual spot at the bar and we ordered our drinks. We hadn't even been seated five minutes when two men, probably a few years older than the two of us, walked over and began talking with us. Addison let them go on with their stories of how two women as beautiful as us didn't need to be sitting at a bar alone, yadda, yadda, yadda, before she looked at them and said, "Oh, I'm sorry, we aren't alone, we're lesbians." Their eyes almost popped out of their heads and on that note they turned and sulked away.

Laughing hysterically, we finished our drinks and followed our waitress to the table. "I didn't think you were in the mood to be picked up tonight," she said sympathetically.

"It's fine, really, I'm okay."

She pulled her eyebrows together and tried to talk low, so people wouldn't hear her, "Reagan, its okay to be upset, you don't have to shield yourself from your feelings, not around me at least."

I leaned back against the booth and took a deep breath before I laid it all out for her. "I get that, I really do, trust me it would be so much easier if I just stayed at home and cried for weeks and weeks, but I can't. I'm working on one of the biggest projects of my career and I don't have time to dwell on something that I cannot change. Cole made his decision and we both have to live with the consequences. Does it hurt? Of course, it hurts to wake up, to eat, to sit here and talk to you, even to say his name, but I can't think about that.

"I've got to think about what's best for me, and dwelling on the fact that he broke my heart into a trillion pieces isn't doing anything positive for me. I, of all people, know life can suck, but I also know you can't stop living because you were dealt a shitty hand of cards. You lock it up as far out of your mind as you can get it, you plant that smile back on your face, and get on with your life." I took a giant gulp of my drink, needing it to finish. "It sucks, it really does, but I've done it before and I can do it again. I just have to focus on work and making partner and I'll be fine. Before Cole that was my sole focus, so I'll just go back to that."

Addison looked truly sad for me. "I just don't want you to be sad. I know you better than anyone else, and I know you're smiling, but your eyes tell a different story, other people may not notice it, but I've been your best friend since we were born and I know when you're putting on a front."

She definitely had me pegged, after twenty seven years I would imagine so. "Don't worry about me, I'll be fine, it's just fresh, give me a week or so and I promise my eyes will smile, too."

She leaned across the table and pulled me into a tight hug as she whispered, "I hope so."

Chapter Sixteen

Heading into the office the next morning I felt confident and ready to get my head back in the game. When I passed through the glass doors of our lobby, our receptionist greeted me, "Good morning, Ms. Larson. Killer outfit." I smiled as I passed her, heading towards my office.

My assistant followed me in as I swept past her desk. "Feeling better, I see." she observed, as I tossed my purse on my couch and headed for my computer, sitting down behind my desk.

"Yes, must have been a twenty-four hour bug." Pulling up my calendar I asked, "What's on the agenda for today?"

She fiddled with her iPad as she reviewed my calendar with me, "9:15 you and Graham have an appointment to discuss Imperial Park prior to your 10:30 meeting with Mr. Conrad." I felt my stomach flip. I pinched the bridge of my nose, taking in a slight breath of air. I should have known things wouldn't have slowed down just because we weren't together anymore; the project still had to go on. "There is a luncheon you are signed up for with the city at 11:30," she went on, "and after that you are clear, until 3, when you have an appointment with a Heather Maxwell."

"Excuse me!" I exclaimed a little louder than usual.

Peering back at her iPad my assistant looked over everything again, "3p.m… Heather Maxwell, is something wrong?" she asked.

I leaned back in my chair and laughed an infuriated laugh. "Cancel the 3p.m. and in the future, don't ever put that name on my calendar again, or anyone's in this firm for that matter."

"Is everything ok?" she asked, looking confused.

"Perfect, just keep that woman out of this firm. Trust me when I say it would do more harm than good." And at that she nodded and headed back to her desk, just as Graham walked in for our 9:15.

Adjusting my outfit in the mirror, I tried my best to compose myself. *You've got this, Reagan, cool and collected, just get in and get it over with, you've already gone over everything with Graham and he knows he is to deal directly with Cole and report back to you.*

I reached for the conference room door and pulled it open, scanning the room. Graham had done great, pulling together every associate on our team for the meeting. The more people we had in the room the less likely Cole would try and discuss anything other than business. Straightening my shoulders and lifting my chin I walked in exuding confidence, taking my seat at the head of the oversized conference room table. Speaking to my team first, I thanked them for gathering on such short notice. And then it was time to address Cole. The lump in my throat began to grow, but I forced it back down as I looked up into those big golden eyes I had fallen so madly in love with.

"Mr. Conrad," I addressed him as I watched him lean back in his chair crossing his arms over his massive chest, "I need to inform you that I have been placed on a few other projects, and I will no longer be your point of contact on

Imperial Park." His brows furrowed as he sucked in a heavy breath. "Graham will be able to take care of any needs you may have, if there are any problems he and I will discuss them and he will then report back to you." Cole stood up and paced in front of the glass windows of the large conference room. "Is there something wrong, sir?" I asked trying to keep it together.

Looking over his shoulder at me I could see the terrifying combination of both rage and pain that was forming behind his eyes. He walked back to the table, and he rested his hands firmly on the edge, looking at the team Graham had assembled. "Would you all give us a few moments to discuss these changes privately?" he demanded, even if it was phrased as a question. My team rose out of their seats and exited the conference room. *So much for no man left behind, great job, Graham.*

As the last person pulled the door closed behind him Cole collapsed into the chair next to me, looking completely defeated. "Reagan why are you doing this?"

I stood at his accusation, "I'm not doing anything, Cole. I'm busy and there are several projects that I need to focus on, you know exactly what's at stake for me. I can't do it all by myself, that's why I put Graham in charge, he's second best to me and I know he'll get the job done properly."

He reached for my hand and I retreated. "I don't give a damn about who's working on the project, Reagan. Hell, I'll pull the plug on all of this right now if you want me to. I mean you and me, why are you doing this to you and me? You won't even give me the opportunity to explain."

It was almost impossible to hold back the tears, but I forced them away, knowing full well I couldn't fall apart in front of him. "I just can't, Cole. I don't want your explanation, I don't care about it. I just need you to respect my wishes, and right now the only wish I have is for you to stay as far away from my life as humanly possible."

"But Reagan...."

Interrupting his sentence before he could finish, "no buts, Cole, I'm done." I turned to walk away, but he grabbed my arm, jerking me back against him as he lifted my face, so I was forced to look up into his eyes.

"Just hear me out, you don't understand what happened…"

Once again, before he could finish I jabbed my finger into his chest, shutting him up. "No! You need to understand… I gave you everything I had, all of me. I trusted you to love and protect me and you did the complete opposite. You destroyed me, Cole. I've never felt pain as bad as I have these past couple of days and it's all your fault." I took a deep breath. "Actually, you know what, it's not your fault, it's my fault. I was the one stupid enough to think the playboy had actually fallen in love with me."

"I do love you, Reagan. I love you more than anything on this earth."

I pulled myself out of his arms as I walked towards the doors, stopping to glance back at him. "You don't even know what love is." His face fell into his hands. "And, Cole, please do me one favor, tell your girlfriend to stay off of my calendar. I have no reason to ever see that woman again and I'd appreciate it if she didn't try to come to my place of business." His eyes looked up, confused as I stormed out of the conference room leaving him there, all alone, just like he'd done to me.

Chapter Seventeen

Leaving Cole alone in the conference room drained me of every emotion I had. I compensated by forcing myself straight into my work. *Contracts don't talk back.* I thought as I focused on a new project I'd requested. I spent the next several days in the office. I'd get in around 6 a.m. and leave around midnight. It made the few hours I had to myself -which I'd mostly spent asleep- more tolerable. I was getting back into the groove of things and finally not constantly thinking about Cole.

Addison was worried I wasn't really dealing with the situation, so much so she even had her mom swing by the office to check in on me. "Reagan, honey, are you holding up okay?" She asked, as she wrapped her arms around me, hugging me tight.

"Absolutely, I've just been super busy here at work. We have so many projects going on and I'm trying to juggle all of them, did you hear I'm being considered for partnership?"

I could see both the excitement and concern in her eyes as she replied, "Yes, Addison told me all about it. We're so thrilled, your mom and dad would have been so proud of you," she took a deep sigh before going on, "but, Reagan, we really are concerned, you can't just push this entire thing with Cole to the wayside, sweetie. You have to deal with it, have you talked to him about it? I know it's really none of my business, but you're like a daughter to me, and I don't want to see you hurting. If you no longer want to be with him, that's fine, and we'll all stick by your decision, but I want you to make sure that is truly what you want before you call it quits for good."

A smile came across my face as she spoke to me, a real smile. And it occurred to me in that moment that I hadn't smiled since the evening of the party, before everything happened with Cole and Heather. I loved Addison's parents and in that very moment, as much as it ripped my heart out to even hear Teresa say Cole's name, I was thankful that, even though, my mom was gone, I had someone like Teresa who was there for me, no matter what. I contemplated my response before I answered, if there was anyone who could call my bluff it was Teresa, she had known me since I was a born, and she always knew when Addison and I weren't telling the truth, so I did my best to sound believable.

"It's hard, really hard, I have no desire to do anything, but figure out a way to make that night disappear, but I can't. I love Cole, and up until that evening, I really thought he could be the man I'd spend the rest of my life with, but seeing him with Heather proved that his bachelor ways are still lingering in his system. And really, who am I to force him to change the way he has been his entire adult life? I may not like it, but in all honesty, it's probably better it happened sooner rather than later. I just can't have anything jeopardize my career right now, and dealing with him, constantly wondering where he is and who he is with, I won't be able to focus. Before he came into my life I was perfectly content being single, I had priorities and I'm not going to change them for a man.

"I hate that it played out this way, but there isn't anything I can do to fix it, he was in the wrong, not me. And as much as I'd like to try and deal with it and him, I just can't take that chance right now. I really am okay, I promise. I hurt, my heart mostly, it literally aches, but it's all part of life. You just have to live and let live. I'm glad I at least got to experience all of the good with him. Maybe one day, when he meets someone new, this will be a reminder to not screw up." She sat across from me taking in my every word. *Come on, if I ever needed an Oscar award for my acting skills it was right now.* She got more comfortable in her chair as she thought about what she was going to say and by the look in her eyes I could tell I was busted.

"Let me tell you something not too many people know," she paused getting up to close my office door. After she sat back down across from me she went on, "when Addison was five years old Theo was on a business trip in Italy. He had been gone for almost two months and we were missing him terribly, so we decided to pack our bags and surprise him. When we landed we went straight to the hotel to see him, the bellhop took us up to his suite and let us in, trying to assist in the surprise. When we walked into his suite I heard a woman's voice coming from the other side of his bedroom door. I sat Addison down on the couch and told her to play with her baby doll, until I could figure out what was going on.

"When I walked into his suite he was in bed with another woman." I gasped, completely shocked. From what I had always remembered Theo and Teresa were just as happy as Mom and Dad, I'd never imagined they'd been through something like this. Teresa held her hands up as she went on, "It was utterly devastating, especially knowing our five year old daughter was sitting right on the other side of the door. Of course, my first reaction was to take Addison back to the airport and meet with my attorney as soon as we made it back to the states, but that obviously wasn't what happened. Addison ran into the arms of her father, as his mistress snuck out of the back door, and as I watched how happy she was seeing her daddy I knew I couldn't allow this to break up our family. I wouldn't do that to my daughter, she deserved to grow up in a happy home. It took a long time for Theo and me to work things out, but we did and I can tell you, he never repeated his mistake again after that day.

"Now, I realize that Theo and I had a lot more riding on our relationship than you and Cole, but I just want you to realize, people make mistakes. It's not up to us to judge them, rather we have to decide if we are willing to forgive them. It's not easy, trust me, it can be one of the most difficult things you'll ever have to do, but in the end it could possibly bring you the most joy you could ever imagine. I couldn't possibly imagine having shared my life with anyone else. Like I said, it wasn't easy, but once I fully forgave him it was as if it never happened and we have truly lived happily ever after since."

I sat there in shock, staring wide eyed at Teresa. She stood up and pulled me into a hug. "Now, don't go feeling sorry for me, I made my choice many, many years ago and it was the best decision I've ever made. There isn't a day that doesn't go by that I don't know Theo loves me with his entire heart, trust me, he's spent the last twenty some years making up for his mistake."

I tried to hug her back, still in shock. "Does Addison know?" I asked, hoping I wouldn't have to feel like I was keeping a secret from my best friend.

"Yes, I had this same conversation with her when her first college boyfriend cheated on her, luckily she didn't listen to her momma with that one." I chuckled as Teresa held me at arm's length. "Just remember, once in a lifetime love is hard to come by, when you have it, you have to work hard at it and hold onto it as tight as you possibly can." She kissed my cheek. She headed towards the door, looking over her shoulder, she stopped and smiled. "That boy's working hard to win you back, you know, he loves you Reagan, he really does." And at that she left. I sat there wondering what in the heck she meant when she said he was working hard to win me back. But before I had time to really think about it my phone chimed, it was Addison.

YOU'RE COMING OVER FOR THANKSGIVING, RIGHT?

Holy crap, was it Thanksgiving already? I thought, pulling up my calendar. Not yet, but it would be in two days. I quickly responded back to her.

OF COURSE, ARE YOU TAKING IT ON THIS YEAR OR ARE YOU LEAVING IT UP TO YOUR PARENTS AGAIN?

I'M GOING TO GIVE IT A SHOT. CASE WANTED TO HAVE IT AT OUR HOUSE THIS YEAR, LUCKILY HIS MOM AND MINE ARE COOKING, I JUST HAVE TO HOST.

WHO'S ALL COMING OVER?

MOM, DAD, MY IN-LAWS, A FEW OF CASEY'S COUSINS.

COUSINS? WHICH ONE'S EXACTLY?

CONNOR, CADE........COLE.

I dropped my phone onto my desk. Of course, Cole would be there. His parent's lived hundreds of miles away, he'd need someone to spend the holidays with if he wasn't visiting California. A few minutes later my phone chimed again.

I CAN UN-INVITE HIM IF YOU WANT?

"Seriously!" I shouted out loud, thankful no one else in

the office heard me. "Oh perfect, make me look like the big bad guy for making Cole spend Thanksgiving alone, while the rest of his family is all together." I shot back a text ending the conversation.

IT'S FINE, ONE DAY WITH HIM WON'T KILL ME, I HOPE.

Chapter Eighteen

Looking in the mirror, I was totally pleased with my wardrobe choice. The cool weather had blown in early and I was thankful, it meant I got to put my boots and scarves to good use. Adjusting my scarf, I smiled at the finished product, dark denim jeans that rested snug on my hips, a loose coral sweater, my favorite leopard scarf, knee high brown boots, and gold chunky jewelry. The combination was one of my favorites, a mixture of sweet and sassy, yet sexy enough, sure to get Cole's attention and make him stare. I'd thought long and hard for two days about Teresa's advice, and I'd finally decided it was time to let Cole explain what really happened that night, and if I was going to spend more than five minutes with him I wanted to ensure his undivided attention would be focused on me.

Running into the kitchen, I grabbed the dessert I'd picked up from my favorite Italian bakery the night before. Three dozen stuffed cannoli and full tray of tiramisu, not your usual Thanksgiving dessert, but it had been tradition in my house since before I was born, and something I'd continued every year, even after my parents passed. I got everything settled into the car and took off towards Addison and Casey's house.

After I pulled into their oversized driveway, I studied all the cars that were parked in front of the house, looking for Cole's black SUV. There was one similar, but it wasn't his. Part of me was excited I'd beat him there and part of me wasn't. The part that needed a glass of wine was definitely glad I'd arrived first.

I opened the door and stepped into the house, the smell of all things Thanksgiving sent my nose into overdrive. Case was on the phone in the foyer when I walked in. He came right over to me and hugged me, still talking to whoever was on the other line of the phone. I whispered, "Happy Thanksgiving," as he smiled and pointed towards the kitchen. Laughing to myself while I walked away, my first thought was Addison would kill him if she knew he was on the phone -probably talking business- on a holiday. I came around the corner and the house was full, all of Casey's family was there including his cousin's and their girlfriends, the Cartwright's were there and even Addison's uncle, aunt and their families. It was a packed house.

"Happy Thanksgiving, everyone," I shouted over the commotion of multiple voices holding conversations. They all turned in my direction and I was greeted with shouts from all over, "Happy Thanksgiving!" I set the dessert's down as Addison ran over to my side. She looked too cute in her fall attire covered by an apron that read, "Taste Tester" in hot pink. I chuckled lightly, knowing she hadn't cooked anything that would be served for dinner tonight.

She pulled me into a tight hug whispering into my ear, "Don't worry he's not here yet." I smiled at my best friend, as I took the wine glass out of her hand and gulped down her entire glass in one breath.

She laughed at me before yelling for Casey, "Babe, we need more wine. I need a refill and Reagan needs a glass....or maybe a bottle!" She winked at me just before I was passed off to her parents.

Two full hours and four glasses of wine had passed by the time I'd finally made it around to everyone. They'd all wanted to make sure I'd been okay since the breakup. It was torturous, I was grateful to have people who cared so much about me, but it was still making me crazy as I had to explain that I was okay to each person. I felt like grabbing a megaphone and screaming, "Yes, Cole broke my heart, but don't worry, I'm okay. I've been through worse. I'll survive."

Addison and Casey were sneaking into the box cannoli when I snuck up on the both of them. "Get out of there!" I hollered in a deep voice as the two of them jumped, guiltily turning around, laughing hysterically when they realized it was me. Case kissed Addison's lips, licking the leftover cannoli filling that was proof they'd gotten into dessert before dinner.

"So, where is he?" I asked, filling my wine glass, yet again.

Case looked at his phone. "I'm not sure, you want me to call him?"

"I guess," I responded hesitantly.

Casey scrolled through his address book and then hit Cole's name. I leaned up onto my tiptoes, pressing my ear as close to Casey's phone as I could possibly get it, to ensure I could hear their entire conversation, a grin coming over my face as I heard him answer, "Hey, man, what's up?" *Oh how I'd missed that deep voice.*

"Where in the hell are you? Everyone is here, you're the only person we're waiting on."

"I'm sorry, I'm going as fast as I can. I had to come down to one of the construction sites, there was an emergency. We're wrapping up in a few minutes, I should be there in about half hour."

"Alright, hurry up, I'm hungry as hell."

"Is Reagan there?" My heart skipped a beat at the sound

of my name on his tongue and I instantly held my breath.

"Yeah, she's here"

"How does she look?"

Case looked me up and down, "gorgeous as ever."

I heard Cole sigh. "Fuck man, is she purposefully trying to kill me?" Case just laughed as Cole finished, "I guess in her eyes I deserve it. Alright, let me go so I can finish up. I'll be there as soon as I can, make sure I have the seat next to her, even if she throws a fit." My heart skipped again. "Will do, I'll see you in a bit." And at that he hung up.

I threw my arms around Casey's neck. "I love you, Casey Conrad!"

He squeezed me and said, "Love you, too, babe."

An hour had passed since Case hung up with Cole and all the guests were beginning to get antsy. "Honey, when are we going to serve dinner?" Teresa asked Addison.

"We're waiting on Cole. He should be here any minute."

"Well, can we at least start getting the main course on the dining room table? We can't hold everyone up for one person."

"Yeah, sure, Mom, Reagan and I will help you. Babe, call Cole again, find out where in the heck he is." Case got on his phone, and Addison and I went into the kitchen to help get everything on the table.

We'd fully set the table when Case came into the dining room. "I've tried four times, it keeps ringing through to voicemail. I guess we can just go ahead and get started without him and when he gets here he can join us. I'm sure he wouldn't want us to wait on his behalf."

"Alright, everyone, let's get seated and enjoy this wonderful meal." Teresa shooed all of us towards the table.

Dinner was spectacular, Addison was lucky she had such wonderful cooks in her family. She and Casey would never have to go without amazing homemade meals. Everyone had stuffed themselves as full as the turkey when Case asked if I would grab the cannoli.

"Casey, you just ate three plates, I think the cannoli can wait until we've cleared the table." His mother scolded. I laughed, getting up to grab them.

Walking into the kitchen, I heard Casey's phone ring. "Dude, where in the hell are you he asked?" I smiled, assuming it was Cole telling him he was on his way. Plating the cannoli, Teresa came in to help me.

"You seem better today." She smiled as I opened the box that had the tiramisu in it.

"I am, I thought a lot about what you said. I'm going to talk to Cole tonight and get down to the bottom of it. I love him, and miss him so much, I wish he'd just hurry up and get here, so I could tell him that."

"I'm glad you thought about it, I know he is going to be elated." She smiled and pulled me into a hug, grabbing the tray of cannoli. I picked up the dish holding the tiramisu and followed her back in towards the dining room.

"I hope that was Cole telling you he's almost here, what in the world has taken him so long?" I asked, looking up just in time to notice the entire table staring at me, looks of sheer horror etched on all of their faces. I instantly realized Casey's mom crying into Mr. Conrad's shoulder, Addison couldn't even look at me. I knew this had to be bad. I turned directly towards Casey and noticed that his eyes were in a losing battle with the tears that were welling up inside of them. My heart stopped beating as I sucked in what seemed like my last breath of air. "Case, what's wrong?" I begged with a shaky voice. No one said a word; they all just looked around at each other. *What is wrong, what the hell happened, where is Cole, why isn't anyone saying anything?!* I screamed from the inside.

Finally, Casey stood up, gripping the chair, to hold himself up. "Reagan, its Cole" he said, a tear sliding down his cheek. And as if I was moving in slow motion my body went limp; the tiramisu slipping from my fingers crashing loudly onto the floor, shattering at my feet.

Chapter Nineteen

I couldn't tear my eyes away from Casey, even though, the pain in his stare was beginning to make me nauseous. My body began trembling as Teresa came over and wrapped her arms around my shoulders, trying to make me sit down, but my legs wouldn't move. It's as if a magnet was holding my feet to that very spot. Finally, words escaped my mouth, entirely on their own, as my brain had already turned to mush. "What happened?" I whispered.

I could feel the stares of the entire room, peering into me as Casey began to speak. "Cole," he hesitated, "he's been in an accident." My heart sunk into the pit of my stomach. I closed my eyes, trying to hold back the tears. Casey's voice went on, "That was the hospital. I was the last number dialed on his cell phone, so they called me. They suggested that we get there right away," he paused again and I could hear the anguish in his voice, "it's not looking good, Reagan." And with those five words, the identical words the doctor used before my parents had been taken away from me, my heart burst into a million shattered pieces.

Addison was at my side, forcing me into a hug, as the

tears began to spill down my cheeks. My breathing began to accelerate, until I heard Cole's words in my head, *'Calm down, we've really got to work on these panic attacks.'* The sound of his voice echoed in my head, I realized that I needed to get it together and get to the hospital. I could break down later, but right now I needed to be strong for Cole. "Addison, get the car, we need to get to the hospital now."

She ran towards the garage and I grabbed Casey's hand, pulling him towards the front door. Addison was waiting for us, so we jumped into the SUV and she hightailed it towards the hospital. Pulling into the emergency room bay, Addison shouted for both of us to get out, "Go! I'll park the car and find you, just get to Cole." Casey and I jumped out of the SUV and ran straight to the nurses' station.

"I'm Casey Conrad, my cousin Cole Conrad was just brought in, I need to get to him. Can you please tell me where he is?" I instantly noticed her eyes widen as she looked to the other nurse, and panic began to rise inside of me all over again.

Pushing it back down for Cole, I leaned over the counter. "Please, can you just tell us where he is? We have to get to him."

The nurse hit a few buttons on her computer and sighed before responding, "He's currently still in surgery. As soon as the doctor is available, I'll let him know the family has arrived." She paused, it looked like she was trying to gather her thoughts, "Would you two like to wait in one of our private waiting rooms?" she asked sympathetically. *No! No! No! This isn't good; they don't give you a private waiting room unless they think their patient isn't going to make it. Tell her no. Case. PLEASE TELL HER NO!!!*

"Yes, please, and ma'am, as soon as you hear anything, would you be sure to let us know?"

"Absolutely." She forced a smile as she led us down a long hallway towards a private waiting room.

Casey collapsed in the recliner chair, while I paced back and forth in the waiting room. After Addison found us, she and Casey were sitting together talking. I tried to listen to what he was telling her, but everything sounded as if Charlie Brown's teacher was speaking. After an hour of wearing a hole in the floor, I decided to sit down in the corner, away from everyone who had arrived after us. I pulled my knees up to my chest, unlocked my phone in search of the "Cole" folder I'd stored away in my online file system. Clicking on his name opened a world of memories, and after flipping through picture after picture I'd finally found what I was looking for.

I turned the volume down low, so I would be the only one to hear it before opening the video. And there he was, the love of my life, standing atop of the Grand Canyon. He'd made sure to take a half day of his business trip to Phoenix and go see one of the places he'd wanted to visit since he was a little kid. Tears pricked my eyes as his voice came over the speakers of my iPhone.

"Hey, baby, can you believe I'm here? It's incredible, I've never seen anything like it. Well, other than you, of course. I miss you, so much, and I wish you were here to enjoy this with me. We'll plan a trip back, don't worry. I can't wait to get home to you. It's only been a day and a half, but I feel like it's been a year. Anyway, I hope you aren't working too hard. I'll be home soon to fix it, if you are. I love you, so much."

I touched his face as the movie played over my phone, the tears slowly sliding down my cheeks. As soon as I brought my finger to the screen to start the video over again, the door of the waiting room swung open and the doctor walked in. I stood up as quickly as I possibly could, running straight to Casey's side, he wrapped his arm around my shoulder. "I assume you are the family of Mr. Conrad?"

Casey spoke for all of us in his answer, "Yes, can you please tell us what's going on?"

"Mr. Conrad was in a severe accident at one of his

development sites. He was exiting the building from the seventeenth floor when the freight elevator collapsed, while he was inside of it." I cringed, hiding my face into Casey's side. He instantly held me tighter. "I don't have much more regarding the actual accident as I do the surgery. When Mr. Conrad arrived our team began treating him for a traumatic brain injury, as well as several broken bones and collapsed lungs. It wasn't looking good in the beginning as his brain continued to swell, but, thankfully, we were able to get that under control and begin accessing the rest of his injuries.

"We've had to put him into a medically induced coma in order to allow his brain to continue to heal. We'd hoped we could avoid this, but his body was working too hard. This will allow him to rest while the swelling subsides. We're going to continue to monitor his progress, but we want you all to be aware that the next forty-eight hours are very critical, as the hemorrhaging of the blood in the brain hasn't fully stopped." I felt Casey's body move as he spoke to the doctor, but I again was only hearing muffled voices as I clung to his side, tears rolling down my face.

The doctor began speaking again, "Of course, we'll ensure he has everything he needs. They're transporting him now to the Intensive Care Unit. Once he has arrived in his room, the only visitors he'll be allowed to have are immediately family members, and there's a two person limit per visit." My eyes widened as I heard the words immediate family repeat in my head. *There is no way in hell you are keeping me from being in that room, I don't give a damn what your rules are.* I thought as the doctor asked if the first two visitors would like to walk with him to the room.

"Yes," Casey said.

But the doctor went on, "And I'm sorry, but I have to ask your relation to Mr. Conrad."

"I'm his brother and this is his fiancé," he answered, pulling me closer to his side, the doctor looking at me for the first time with sympathy in his eyes.

He took a deep breath as he went on, "Okay, if I could just have both of your I.D.'s, I'll get you the proper hospital passes and be back in just a minute." We handed him our I.D.'s and he exited the room.

Casey's mom walked up to both of us, taking her son's free hand. "Honey, I'm not trying to cause any trouble here, but don't you think your father should go back with you first? Cole is his nephew, and I'm sure your aunt and uncle would want to hear how he is doing from your father." My head shot up as I glared at her from under Casey's arm.

"No, Mom, you and Dad can go in after Reagan and me, but we're going in first. That'll give you time to call Uncle Harrison and Aunt Candice. They need to get on a flight and get here."

"But son…"

"Mom, I said no." Casey said sternly. The doctor walked back into the waiting room, handed us our hospital stickers and asked us to follow him as he led both Casey and me down the white sterile hallway.

Chapter Twenty

Walking through the doors of the ICU my stomached clenched into a thousand knots, taking in all of the rooms that were filled with patients. The doctor stopped in front of Room 8486, turning to face me and Casey before he opened the door. "I need to warn you, he's hooked up to a lot of machines and his body is pretty bruised up. It's possible he can hear you, so don't act frightened when you see him, just talk to him like you normally would. The calmer you remain, the less stressed Cole will be and, right now, we don't need any stress on his brain. If you need anything just let the nurses know and they'll get in contact with me."

"Thank you so much," Case replied as the doctor walked off. "You ready?" he asked, looking down at me.

I froze, unable to speak as thoughts of everything that could possibly go wrong ran through my brain. "I don't think I can do this, Case," I whispered.

His arms wrapped around me, cradling me right up against his chest. "I know this is difficult, but you have to, your voice is the first one he would want to hear, you have to do this for him." He pushed the door open and stepped in, pulling me in behind him.

Looking up from the floor I saw my everything lying there in a hospital bed. I started at his toes working my way up, counting each bandage, bruise, or stitch that hadn't been there the last time I'd seen him. His body was black and blue from being tossed like a rag doll in the fall. Needles, which connected to tubes that led to hanging bags, were inserted and taped to the tops of his hands. His chest was bare of clothes, but covered in gauze. I winced at the thought of what the lacerations looked like underneath. Finally, I'd made it to his beautiful face. Behind the clear ventilator hose protruding out of his mouth, numerous staples sealing a deep gash on his hairline, and the dark purple sheen of bruises I saw the man I'd fallen so madly in love with.

Catching my breath, I ran to his side and reached for his hand, even as he lay there lifeless in the hospital bed, a spark still flew through my body at the touch of his skin. The tears began to fall harder as I moved my left hand up towards his head, smoothing his hair as gently as possible. I leaned in and lightly placed a kiss on his forehead, my body trembling as my mouth touched his skin. Lingering there for a moment, I could still smell the scent of cologne on his body. Bringing my face down towards his I kissed his cheek and whispered into his ear.

"Hi, honey," I whispered, trying to compose my emotions. "I'm here, it's me, Reagan." Kissing his cheek again, I went on whispering, so only he and I could hear what I was saying. "Baby, I'm so sorry for everything I put you through. I know this isn't the ideal time to talk about it, but you just need to know, I don't care what happened. The only thing I'm concerned about is that you know I love you. You're the person I want to spend the rest of my life with. You've got to get better so I can tell you that, please, Cole. I can't live without you." The sobs began escaping my throat and Casey quickly pulled me into a hug.

"Shhhh… you can't cry like this, sweetie, not in here. I know it's difficult and I'm sure it's a hell of a lot harder for you, but we've got to keep calm for him."

"I'm trying, Case, I really am, but what if he doesn't make it, what if I never have the chance to tell him I love him, again?"

He squeezed me tighter. "Cole is a fighter. He knows you love him, and that alone will have him fighting harder than he's ever fought before, trust me Reagan, he loves you. He's not leaving this earth any time soon, especially not before he has the chance to make things right with you, I can promise you that." Casey's words reassured me, but I was still terrified. Having my entire reason for existence grasping for life before my eyes was unbearable.

We both sat there on each side of him, for over an hour, just talking to him. Casey finally lightened the mood and began joking with Cole. The nurse came in to check on him as Casey was telling him about one of their cousins girlfriends, "You should've seen her, man, I swear he picked her up at a strip joint. Mom's mouth hit the floor when she walked in. Addison had to give her a change of clothes before everyone else got there." I laughed as Casey finished.

"Do that again," the nurse exclaimed, looking over at me.

"Do what?" I asked, confused.

"Anything, laugh, talk, whatever, just do it again."

I looked at Casey, wondering what in the heck she was asking me to do as he shrugged his shoulders. "Umm, I'm not sure what to say, is there something specific you need?"

She pointed at one of the monitors that was connected to wires attached Cole's body, "Watch the screen, do you see how the vitals are lower while I'm talking?" She looked to Casey. "Say something to him, anything."

Casey stood up and leaned towards Cole. "Hey, man, when are you going to wake up?"

The monitor remained the same and the nurse looked

back to me. "Your turn."

I stood up, still holding Cole's hand. "Hey, baby, I'm not really sure what to say, but the nurse suggested I talk, so I'm talking, I love you so…" and as those three words came out of my mouth the lines on the monitor started moving up. My eyes widened as they flew to the nurse and then to Casey.

"Keep talking," she whispered.

"I love you, baby, I'm right here by your side, and I'm not going anywhere, so rest as long as you need to, but just know, when you wake up it's back to me and you." The lines were going crazy on the monitor.

"He likes the sound of your voice, every time you talk his vitals rise."

"Is that okay, or should I not talk so much?"

She laughed. "It's perfectly fine, and a good sign, if you ask me. It means his brain is working to heal itself, which is exactly what we want."

"Does this mean he can hear what we are saying?" I needed to know if he knew how I felt about him.

"It just depends, we have found out after patients have come out of coma's that they heard everything that was said, and some never heard anything. But I can tell you this much, whether he knows what you're saying or not, he recognizes the sound of your voice, and that in itself is huge," She replied, walking out of the room.

A smile grew across my face as I looked to Casey. "Can you believe he knows it's me?"

He grinned. "Of course I can, you're all that man thinks about. Why wouldn't he know the sound of your voice?" Casey stood up and walked over to me, resting his hands on my shoulders. "Reagan, he loves you, he never stopped. Trust me, there's more to the story than you think. I'm glad you are giving him a second chance." Kissing the top of my head he walked towards the door. "I'm going to go report back to the family, let them know how he is doing. I'm sure my mom and dad will want to come back, but I'll send them one at a time making sure they only stay for ten to fifteen minutes. And please, don't let anyone who comes back here try and pressure you into letting someone else come in. Cole would want you here at his side over anyone else. Text me if anything changes, as soon as everyone gets to see him I'll come back in." I smiled at Casey as he walked out of the hospital room.

When Casey left I knew it would only be a matter of minutes before another family member came in to visit with Cole, so I took the little alone time we had to talk to him more. Kissing his forehead, again, I rubbed his cheek with my fingers. "You know there are so many things I haven't told you yet, like when Addison and Case got married, I pictured me and you walking down the aisle together as husband and wife. And whenever one of my girlfriends finds out they are having a baby, my first thought is what a wonderful father you'll be. There are so many things we still have to do together, Cole. Your mom was right when she talked about the two of us that night, I may have been terrified in that moment of what the future held, but I know now there is no other future I could ever ask for. You and me, that's what's meant to be" I kissed him again as a light knock came from outside his room.

Chapter Twenty-One

Family members were in and out of the room for the next several hours, taking turns, allowing me to stay at his side the entire time. Apparently more had arrived since I'd been back here. Casey finally came back in and I noticed he was carrying a bag with him.

"Visiting hours are wrapping up here in about five minutes, so we're going to head home. Addison brought a bag of necessities for you, knowing you aren't going to leave his side. She said if you need anything else just text her and she will run it by."

I stood up and hugged Casey. "Thank you for everything, Case."

He smiled. "Get some rest tonight. Staying up all night, wondering if he is going to wake up won't do you any good."

Damn, he knows me too well. "I'll try my best."

"And if anything changes, please call me. I don't care what time it is." I nodded my head as he turned and left the room. And, finally, I felt able to relax. I hadn't spent more than five minutes alone with Cole in God knows how long, and tonight was the first time in weeks I'd be able to spend the entire night with him.

Looking through the bag Addison packed for me, I found everything I could have possibly needed. I grabbed my pajamas and my overnight bag and walked into the bathroom. I quickly took a shower, washed my face, and brushed my teeth before slipping into my pajamas. Grabbing a blanket and pillow out of the closet, I walked over to Cole's bed. There was just enough room for me to squeeze in next to him. I knew the minute the night nurse came in to check on him she'd probably make me move, but until then I was going to be right where I needed to be, as close to in his arms as I could possibly get.

Adjusting Cole's right arm so the wires weren't in my way, I slowly climbed into the hospital bed. I was moving with every ounce of caution I had in me, watching every wire and tube that was in the vicinity of where I was laying. Finally settled in, I rested my head on his shoulder and pulled the blanket up to my neck. Reaching out from underneath it, I grabbed his hand and pulled it under the covers with me, so I could hold onto him all night. Kissing his shoulder, I whispered, "Goodnight, love." And for the first time, since I'd left him at the hotel, I slept entirely through the night, with the person I loved most on this earth right by my side.

"Reagan, honey, wake up." I heard through tired ears as I opened my eyes, still cuddled up next to Cole. I looked over my shoulder to find Mr. and Mrs. Conrad were standing at the side of the bed. I smiled at the both of them, as I climbed out of the hospital bed.

"Hi," I whispered, hugging Cole's mom and then his dad, "when did you get in?"

Harrison answered, since Candice had already moved to her son's side. "About half hour ago, we caught the first flight out after we got the call. How's he doing?"

Reaching for Cole's free hand I looked to him, and then back at his father. "They said the first forty-eight hours are the most critical. The doctor hasn't been in yet, so hopefully he'll be here soon and discuss everything with us."

Shortly thereafter, the night nurse walked in. "Well, good morning," she said, looking at me. I smiled. "I was surprised to see you in bed with Mr. Conrad last night. I almost woke you up, but his vitals were dancing again, so I let you sleep."

I blushed as Mrs. Conrad looked to the nurse. "What was dancing?" she asked, looking confused.

The nurse laughed. "His vitals, anytime Reagan would talk to him they would jump around, showing brain activity, which is good for the recovery process. He only does it with her, watch; talk to him, Reagan."

I leaned in closer to Cole. "Good morning, baby, your mom and dad made it. They're here right now, luckily no one knows we are violating the two visitor limit, so we're all three in here with you. Hopefully, your nurse won't rat us out, she seems pretty cool, so I think we'll be okay."

The nurse pointed to the screen. "See that?"

I looked over at Mrs. Conrad and the tears were pouring down her face as she smiled up at me. "That's because this girl is our son's everything." My heart skipped a beat as I turned to Mr. Conrad, not sure I'd heard him correctly. He wrapped his arm around my shoulder, kissing the top of my head. "You know that, right? No matter what happened, he never stopped loving you." Leaning into him, I nodded my head yes as I fought back the tears. The nurse told us the doctor would be in shortly as she left, leaving me in a room with Cole and his parents.

A few minutes after the nurse left us the doctor came in, looking over Cole's chart I noticed there was more hope in his eyes than there had been yesterday. "Well, it looks like he is doing better. We still aren't out of the woods, but if we can make it through the next twenty-four hours with the same progress, I can take him off the meds, so his body can transition out of the coma. We'll continue monitoring his progress and keep you updated. Are there any questions or concerns that you may have?" I couldn't think of anything, but Mr. Conrad had a list he was already going over, making sure Cole was getting the very best treatment.

"I'm going to get out of these pajamas before anyone else arrives." I whispered to Candice, as I grabbed my bag.

The next four days passed so slowly. Cole was still progressing, but a minor setback caused the doctor to leave him in an induced coma for one more day before taking him off of the meds. It had been twenty-four hours since he'd been taken off of the medication and he still hadn't woken up, yet. We were all exhausted, Candice, Harrison, and I had taken shifts staying with Cole. I'd wanted to stay with him every night, but knew it was best to give his parents some alone time with him, also.

I'd just woken up and Harrison was there to relieve me, so I could go home and get cleaned up. "I just spoke to the doctor. He's guessing it'll be another five or six hours based on the speed of his vitals. Why don't you run home, get cleaned up, and head back? Candice is on her way now. That way we're all here when he wakes up."

I nodded hugging him. "I'll be back as soon as I can."

When I got home I took a shower, did my hair and make-up, and put on one of my favorite outfits, knowing Cole would more than likely be waking up today. After I'd gathered a few things to take back with me, I decided to catch up on one of my shows really quick. I needed some time to get my mind off of everything, so each day I came home I'd try to catch up on either reading or one of my shows, today it was my favorite cop series. Sitting down on the couch I vowed to only watch thirty minutes, and then it was back to the hospital.

Opening my eyes, only having imagined dozing off for a few minutes, I noticed the sky was darkening outside. "Shit!" I shouted, jumping off of the couch. Looking at my watch I quickly realized it was almost 7 p.m. "Oh.My.Gosh. I slept all day, this can't be happening." I yelled at myself. I quickly grabbed my bag and ran to my car, checking my phone as I rushed to the hospital. I had several missed calls from Candice and Harrison, even a few from Casey and Addison. No one had left any voicemails, but I had a few texts from Addison.

WHERE ARE YOU?

YOU NEED TO GET HERE, NOW!

My heart sank as I read the last one. "Shit! Please let him be okay."

Pulling into the valet drive thru of the hospital, I jumped out of my car, tossing the attendant my keys. I ran straight for the ICU, running into Casey and Addison on the way there. "Is he okay?" I begged.

They were both smiling. "He's fine, he woke up about an hour ago, he keeps asking for you," Addison replied. I hugged them both, then I ran towards the nurses' station. Recognizing the nurses on duty I shouted before I got there, "Can I go in?" My favorite nurse held her hands up. "Mom and Dad are visiting with him. I'll go tell them you're here, just give me a minute, take a second to catch your breath. You look like you just sprinted a marathon."

"Okay, okay, just hurry, please." She smiled as she jogged towards his room.

Catching my breath I pulled out a compact to assess myself before I went back to his room. Not being able to fully focus, I shoved it back into my purse after a minute of fidgeting with the damn thing. Who gives a shit about what you look like right now, *Reagan, you're about to really talk to Cole for the first time in forever, you think he is going to care what you look like?*

Candice, Harrison, and the nurse came around the corner

all wearing the biggest smiles I'd ever seen on their faces, I ran straight towards them, crashing into Candice and Harrison's arms. Words failed me as they both hugged me as tight as possible. Candice held me at arm's length. "He's waiting for you, sweetie. Take as long as you need, we'll be in the waiting room with Casey and Addison." I hugged them both one last time before rounding the corner. His door was slightly open and from a distance I could see that his bed had been readjusted so he was sitting up.

Chapter Twenty-Two

Pushing the door open all the way, I stood there as those golden eyes I had missed so much peered across the room and locked onto mine. He still looked beaten and battered, but he was awake and the ventilation machine was gone. My hands instantly began to tremble as the tears escaped from deep within. I was stuck in the doorway, standing there crying like a child.

"Hey, don't cry. Come here." He lightly laughed, wincing at the pain it caused. The sound of his voice sent chills through my entire body. My feet began moving towards the bed as he stuck out his hand, reaching for mine. I bypassed his hand entirely, climbing straight into bed with him. Wrapping his arm around me, I nuzzled into his shoulder. He let out a huge sigh. "You have no idea how long I've waited to have you back in my arms." Looking up at his beautiful face, I smiled through tear filled eyes as I placed my hand on his chest, trying not to touch any of the bandages that still remained. We laid there staring into each other's eyes for what seemed like eternity.

Cole rubbed the length of my arm, while I rested next to

him just enjoying being in his arms again. Placing a kiss on top of my head he whispered, "Cat got your tongue?"

Realizing I'd yet to say a word since he'd woken up, I quickly sat up and turned towards him. "No, I'm sorry, I think I'm just taking it all in. I have been so worried about you and now having you here, awake, knowing you are okay, it's just so overwhelming. I'm sorry, I just…I just don't know what to even say. I'm not sure where I should even begin."

He smiled and grabbed my hand "How 'bout a kiss?" I blushed, now also realizing I'd yet to kiss him since he'd woken up. Leaning over him I lightly placed my lips on top of his. My body shivering as his hand reached up and wrapped around the base of my neck, pulling me closer to him, pressing his lips harder against mine. My body was on fire, having yearned for his touch for so long. I was surprised when his tongue slipped into my mouth, but not disappointed at all. My heart was pounding out of my chest as he devoured my mouth, I could hardly breathe, but Cole wouldn't let up, until the machine next to us started screaming. I jumped at the sound of the alarm, fear rushing through my body as I looked him over from head to toe in a panic.

"Are you ok?" I begged. He was lying there eyes closed, lips swollen, panting heavily. "Cole?" I shouted as he began to chuckle.

Nurses burst through the door and were at his side in seconds, checking all of the machines. "What is going on in here? Why is your heart rate monitor screaming?" My favorite nurse asked as I put my hands to my mouth, trying to stifle a giggle when I realized Cole was okay. "Cole, answer me, why is your heart rate elevated?"

He looked over towards me, giggling in the corner then back to her. "Well, ma'am, you see that beautiful young lady over there?" He nodded his head in my direction as I blushed, not even able to imagine what was going to come out of his mouth next. "It's been awhile since I've laid my lips on her mouth, and well to be quite honest with you, I wasn't going to give her a half ass kiss, because I'm cooped up in this damn bed. So that machine you're referring to is only screaming, because that's what happens to my heart every time I kiss her."

Silencing his machine the nurse pointed a finger in my direction. "You know better than that, Reagan, I trust it won't happen again?" Winking at me as she looked back to Cole. "And as for you, buddy, you've been out of it for a few days, so I can't fault you for not obeying the rules up until this point, but from here on out your recovery is top priority. Getting hot and steamy with that little lady over there will just have to wait until you bust out of this joint. You understand?" Cole smiled up at her and nodded his head. I was still in the corner trying to avoid being reprimanded again.

As she walked out of the room, I sat back on the edge of the bed, grabbing Cole's hand and kissing it. "I feel like we just got caught in the act or something. I guess, I better take it easy before she kicks me out of here."

He pulled me in closer to him, quickly kissing my lips. "Oh, you aren't going anywhere, not now that I've finally gotten you back."

His words cut with both excitement and pain. "What's wrong?" he asked, squeezing my hand.

I cringed, not wanting to get into the entire Heather thing, but it was there in my mind all of the sudden, so I figured it was best we just get it over and done with. "I just hate that we had to go through all of that. I know it isn't the time to bring it up, but it killed me Cole, you killed me." I looked away, trying not to get too emotional as I remember the two of them in the elevator together. His heavy sigh brought my eyes back to him as he laid there, eyes closed, silent. *Say something!* I screamed in my head, but he didn't. Silence filled the room for what seemed like forever before he finally spoke.

"Reagan, I know nothing will change your perception of what you saw that night, but I have to tell you it is not what you think. I had no idea she was going to kiss me." As the words rolled off of his tongue I realized in that very moment I couldn't possibly rehash anything that had to do with the past couple of weeks and I held my hands up to Cole forcing him to stop talking.

"I can't, I thought I could talk about it, but I just can't. It was painful enough going through it, hearing it all over again will just rub salt on the wound. I don't even care anymore. I just want to forget it ever happened and never talk about it ever again."

Sinking further into the bed, he looked defeated and I felt terrible for bringing it up in the first place. "I know this is hard for you, but I need to get this off of my chest, so please, just hear me out. Once I'm finished, I promise we never have to talk about it again." He asked, staring up at me again. I nodded as I held my breath, still not ready to relive that night.

"I need you to know I would never do anything to hurt you, Reagan. I'll never forgive myself for putting you through that. There were so many times I tried to explain what happened, but you were so angry and I never got the chance. I couldn't risk pushing you further away. I knew if I told you then that she had come on to me there was no way you would believe me, so I figured respecting your wishes and just leaving you alone would be best, until we could finally take the time to discuss everything."

"I knew Heather always had a crush on me, but I never saw her that way. She was a hard worker, so I just chalked it up to her wanting to go over and above for her job. That night in the hotel she finally realized I was utterly in love with you and she saw it as her last possible chance for an opportunity to be with me, so she took it. Right there in the elevator as I was heading back up to the rooftop to find you. It completely caught me off guard, especially when I saw you standing in the lobby as the elevator doors closed. I promise you that kiss was entirely one sided, it meant absolutely nothing to me. I allowed her to finish out her night for the sake of the party, but I fired her the very next day and I have had absolutely no contact with her since."

"Trust me, I hadn't anticipated having to tell you this way, but regardless, I'm glad I'm finally able to talk to you about it, and we can move past it together." *Breathe, Reagan; it wasn't that bad. You should've known he would never do that to you. You see what happens when you assume and don't let anyone explain, you torture yourself for weeks.*

Relief washed through my body as I felt myself let go of everything that had taken place over the course of the past few weeks. Sliding back into bed with Cole, I'd never felt so complete in my entire life. I rested my head on his chest, as he sucked in a sharp breath. Looking up at him I realized I'd moved too quick and hurt him. "Crap, I'm sorry. I didn't mean to hurt you." I whispered, moving to pull away.

His arm held me tighter, so I couldn't get up. "Don't move, I'm fine, a little sore, but it'd be worse if you got up."

Kissing his chest, I wrapped my arm around his waist, smiling to myself. "I love you, Cole Conrad."

He kissed the top of my head. "I love you, more, Reagan Larson."

Chapter Twenty-Three

With each passing day Cole continued to recuperate in the hospital, finally being moved from ICU after two weeks. Once out of ICU it seemed the visitors never stopped; from colleagues to college buddies, he had a constant flow every day. And the room smelled magnificent, you'd think they'd set him up in the middle of a garden. Each day a new arrangement would arrive, filling the room with vibrant colors and smells that made your senses run wild. The nurses even bought him a mini Christmas tree and decorated it, since it was so close to Christmas.

I was sitting in the corner, answering emails while Cole was in physical therapy when a delivery man walked in carrying another arrangement of flowers. I stood, taking them from his hands and smelling them. They were gorgeous, red and white roses, with a green glitter ribbon wrapped around the vase. Pulling the card from the flowers, I smiled as I saw who it was from.

Hurry up and get him out of there, we are dying to see you both. Morning sickness is kicking my ass already. I wish I could come spend the days with you in the hospital, but there is something about the smell that makes me sick to my stomach. We can't celebrate Christmas without you both, so start bribing those doctors. Love you both,

Addison, Casey and "Bun in the Oven"

I laughed at the nickname they'd given their unborn child.

They'd come to the hospital earlier that week to tell us the news, but before Addison could get it out she'd ran straight for the bathroom and puked her guts out. Casey was talking with Cole, so I followed her into the bathroom, to help her get cleaned up.

"I hate to sound like the nurses, but if you're sick maybe you and Case should come back another day. I really want Cole to get out of here sooner rather than later."

She rinsed her mouth out and looked up at me, smiling. "He can't catch what I have, trust me." She forested her hand on her belly.

My eyes followed her hand. "Oh my gosh, you're pregnant!" I screamed, jumping up and down like a child. Addison was laughing at my reaction as she shook her head yes. I grabbed her and pulled her into a hug.

Casey pulled the bathroom door open, looking at the two of us acting like teenagers who'd just won front row tickets to the Backstreet Boys concert, he chuckled. "I take it you told her?"

I swung around and screamed again, "Yes! Congratulations Case, I'm so happy for the both of you!"

"Told her what?" Cole inquired, not having heard the conversation Addison and I just had thirty seconds earlier in the bathroom.

"Someone tell him, before I do!" I exclaimed, rushing to his side.

Casey pulled Addison into his arms, squeezing her tight as she smiled at Cole and said, "We're having a baby!" I began clapping and jumping up and down again after she told Cole.

I looked over at him; he had a huge smile on his face. "That's incredible, congratulations." He and Casey hugged, as I was at Addison's side.

"Tell me everything, when are you due? How far along are you? Shit, I'm glad one of us is getting laid." We both cracked up laughing as the guys talked about the baby hopefully being a boy.

"Well," she began, "not to sound morbid or anything, but the night Cole was in the accident Casey and I got home. We were exhausted and emotionally drained, but I was just so distraught about the fact that you could possibly be losing the man of your dreams, and it made me so scared to ever lose Case. So one thing led to another, I was crying, he was comforting me and the next thing you know we're doing it four or five times that night. I was on the pill, but between drinking that day and not taking it every day like I should, it just happened."

Laughing at the story I looked at my best friend and joked, "Why does it not surprise me that I was here in the hospital worried out of my mind at the possibility of losing Cole, while my best friend is at home with her husband going to town making a baby?"

Addison slapped my arm. "Oh my gosh, don't say it like that, you make me sound like the worst friend on the planet."

"If the shoe fits." I giggled.

She stuck her tongue out at me and tucked herself under Casey's arm, talking to Cole as I sat down on the bed next to him. "You better hurry up and get out of this hospital, her lack of sexual relations is turning her into a grouch."

He glanced over at me and then replied to Addison, "Trust me, when they finally release me from this prison, I'm going to keep her locked up in my room for the next year."

Placing the flowers on the shelf, Cole walked in from physical therapy, looking at the new bouquet as he kissed my cheek. "Who are these from?" I handed him the card and he smiled. "She misses you."

I miss her too. I thought. "What did the therapist say?"

He wrapped his arms around me, trailing my neck with

kisses, sending shivers down my spine. "She thinks I should be released by Thursday afternoon."

I gasped, not sure I heard him right. Looking at my phone to make sure I knew exactly what day it was, I screamed when I saw the word Wednesday on the top of my iPhone. "Are you kidding me, as in tomorrow afternoon?"

He grinned. "Yes.Tomorrow.Afternoon." Kissing me again between each word. I squeezed my arms around his waist with excitement. "Ouch, not so tight, I'm still broken in some places."

Whoops! "Sorry, I'm just so excited to be able to finally take you home."

Making sure everything was in order that afternoon, we called his parents to come pick up the majority of the things we'd collected over the past month in the hospital. They were elated to hear the good news, and got there as soon as possible. "Is there anything we can do before you come home, grocery shop, get anything specific the doctor thinks you should have?" Candice asked, as she and Harrison gathered our things.

"I think all we need are groceries, other than that we should have everything there already, and if we don't we can get it from downstairs." Cole spoke to his parents, while I continued to gather our things together. The room had transformed into an office/bedroom over the past couple of weeks. Finally, we finished packing everything up. Candice and Harrison said goodbye and took our things back to the hotel.

After taking a shower, I climbed into the hospital bed with Cole. "So, what's the first thing you want to do when you get home tomorrow?" I asked, looking up at him curious to hear his answer. A devilish grin spread across his face as he looked down towards his running shorts. My eyes bulged open at the sight of his erection growing beneath his clothes. "Oh, well… I think we'll have to ask about that, I'm not sure what the doctor would say."

He laughed at my reaction, "too soon?"

I shook my head, "absolutely not, not too soon for me, but possibly too soon for you."

"Oh, I'm up for the challenge," he whispered, pulling me up towards his face, so he could take my mouth. Sliding his tongue past my lips, I let out a soft groan. It seemed like it had been forever since he and I were able to really be together. His hand hitched my leg over his body and he shifted himself, so I was practically on top of him. Wrapping one hand in my hair and the other gripping my ass he lightly tugged my head back, running his tongue over my neck, tracing his way down my collar bone. Doing my best to keep my moans under control, I bit my lip tight as I grasped onto the railings of the bed. Cole's erection was growing underneath me, and I could tell had we not been in this hospital room he would have taken me right then and there.

A cough brought us out of our steamy make out session. Quickly jumping off of Cole's lap I sat by his side, at the same time he rushed to pull the covers and pillow over his lap. "You two never cease to amaze me, I thought I told you about breaking the rules?" Our favorite night nurse from ICU had caught us, again.

Cole laughed nervously as she walked towards the bed. "I hear they're releasing you tomorrow afternoon? I wanted to make sure I came to check on you one last time and say goodbye." She chuckled looking over his charts.

"Does everything look good?" I inquired, trying to take the focus off of what she had just walked in on.

Looking at the both of us, she grinned. "Well, you tell me, from the looks of it you'd never know he was just in a horrific accident a little less than a month ago." I blushed, looking down at my hands that were folded in my lap, sweating.

Before I could answer Cole began speaking to her, "So, when can Reagan and I have sex?" I gasped, completely caught off guard by his question and tried to bury my face in my hands before she could answer.

She laughed loudly, resting her hands on the bedside railing. "You know your body, if it hurts, don't do it. If you aren't aching, then go for it. I wouldn't recommend the crazy stuff right off the bat. This may sound too personal, but I've been with you all for a while, so I'll say it, Reagan on top is probably better because you won't be working as hard." I pulled the covers over my head, completely embarrassed. "Oh, Reagan, don't be embarrassed, I'm a nurse. I've seen and talked about it all. I'm just trying to answer honestly."

She laughed, leaning in to hug Cole. "You two get some rest. You'll get tired quicker when you get home and don't have us waiting on you hand and foot. If you need anything, just give me a call." Placing a card down on the nightstand, she winked at me. "Remember, make sure he's comfortable."

Cole gave her a thumbs up and chuckled. "I knew there was a reason you were my favorite nurse." We all laughed, she hugged me and waved goodbye as she left us in the room alone. "You on top, that's the very first thing I want to do when we get home. Is that okay with you?" I blushed, nodding my head yes as a puddle of heat pooled between my legs.

Chapter Twenty-Four

Stepping out of the elevator into Cole's suite, he smiled and squeezed me closer to his side. "It's good to be home." I closed my eyes, smiling to myself. Taking his hand I led him to the couch to sit down. He'd already overexerted himself, making sure he said hello to all of the staff on his way in.

"Why don't you lie down and relax? I'll grab you some water and put these last few things away, then we can watch a movie." He sat down, and before I knew it he'd pulled me down with him. Letting out a light giggle, I looked up into his beautiful eyes that were flooded with raw desire.

"Movie my ass, all I want to do is get you out of these clothes and on top of my lap." My heart jumped with excitement at his rough whisper. Excited at his eagerness, I threw my legs over him, resting right on top of his lap. His body's reaction to mine sent chills straight down my spine. I leaned closer into his neck, taking his earlobe into my mouth. A deep groan escaped his mouth as his hands worked their way up my sides, leaving a trail of goose bumps behind. He pulled my shirt over my head, discarding it onto the floor. His mouth began devouring my breasts, jerking at the straps of my lace bra, trying to free me for further access.

Leaning my head back, I opened my body further, his mouth lingering on each nipple as he took turns teasing me. The sensation that was beginning to build had been long anticipated. "Oh Cole," I let out a cry in a hoarse voice.

His eyes shot up to mine, relishing in the sound of his name on my lips. "Tell me what you want, baby?" I couldn't speak, the emotions that were raking my body and having not been with him in months had me at a loss for words, so instead of responding back with words, I decided I'd let my body do the talking.

Sliding off of his lap, I stood up and decided I'd slowly remind him of what he'd been missing. Bending over, my breast still exposed from his assault on them just moments ago, I unzipped my knee high boots, keeping my eyes locked on his the entire time. Kicking them off, I ran my hands up my legs and over my thighs. I rested my fingers on the button of my jeans. "Should I keep going?" I asked, smiling at his body's eagerness. He swiftly nodded, as his fingers began to unbutton his shirt, our eyes still locked.

My grin grew bigger as my hands freed the button of my jeans and worked at the zipper, pulling it down until it couldn't go any further. Slowly hooking my fingers through the loops of my jeans, I slowly worked them down my thighs. His eyes followed my every move. Standing in front of him in nothing but my black lace bra and panties he reached his hand out to me, but I shook my head no. Instead, reaching to unhook the clasp of my bra, I pulled it off fully, exposing my breasts.

A gasp escaped Cole's lips as he leaned his head back, closing his eyes. "Baby, you're killing me," he whispered when I bent over and tugged at the button of his shorts. Before I could move past his button he had his shorts undone and around his ankles. Giggling, I reached for his hands and placed them on my hips.

"Are you ready for me?" I asked, never losing sight of his eyes.

"Fuck yes, you have no idea." His eyes hooded with desire.

"Oh, I think I do," I said, slipping my hand inside my panties, wanting to show Cole how ready I actually was. As I worked my fingers further south they were met by a pool of wet heat, moaning I rolled my head to the side, as I traced my most sensitive spot with the pads of my fingertips. Cole's eyes widened to the size of golf balls, and before I knew it, he'd wrapped his arms around my hips, pulled my panties as far to the side as he could get them, and yanked me straight down onto his lap, plunging his throbbing erection as deep inside of me as he could possibly get it. I gasped as he filled me completely, his face sinking into my shoulder as his teeth pulled at my skin. My body instantly began reacting to his every move, reaching for his shoulders I began moving my hips in sync with his thrusts.

I met him thrust for thrust. I could feel him growing larger inside of my body as I held him tight deep within. The moans were now escaping both of our throats as undeniable pleasure was washing over the two of us. Cole's pace continued to speed up, his hands moved all over my body, along with his mouth working its way from my jaw back to my breasts. My breathing began to quicken as he plunged deeper and deeper inside of me.

"Faster, Cole," I shouted, and he picked up the pace. I'd waited for so long to feel him take my body that I didn't want it to ever end, but the sensation was so intense that I needed him to push me over the edge.

"Baby," he said through quick breaths, "come for me" and before the words could fully slip off of his tongue my insides shot off like fireworks, and then Cole's body reacted the same. I could feel him pulsating inside of me and that caused another grand finale inside of my body, my head flew back and my eyes rolled back into my head. Cole's massive arms wrapped around me to keep me on top of him as he finished.

Completely spent I collapsed into Cole's shoulder, our hearts slamming against each other as we came down off of such an intense reaction to each other bodies. I laid there, on his lap with him still fully inside of me, as I tried my best to regain my bearings. Cole's fingers tracing my back as he reveled in what'd just happen. "I feel like I've waited so long to have you back in my arms, to make love to you again."

Looking up into his eyes as a tired smile spread across my face. "Me too," I agreed, kissing his lips. Lifting me off of his lap, he laid down and positioned my body right up next to his, as he reached for a blanket and covered both of our naked bodies.

"Let's get some rest, because this is just the beginning."

I giggled, snuggling up against his chest.

Waking me up a few hours later, Cole proceeded to take me from room to room, bed to bed, until we had managed to fully ravish each other on every ounce of his penthouse suite. It was great to be back here with him, in his arms, enjoying every inch of this place, together. Finally making it to his room, we collapsed on his bed thoroughly exhausted.

"Should I order take out?" I breathed heavily. "I know the nurses would kill me if they knew I let you exert all of that energy and I haven't fed you yet."

He sunk further into his pillow, pulling me closer to his warm body. "Yes, please, I'm starving." Leaving him in bed, I walked into the kitchen to grab the take out menus from his kitchen drawer. Looking through them, I grabbed the black menu, and I called and ordered Cole's favorite dinner, something he'd missed the entire time he was in the hospital. I quickly ran to his room and jumped in the shower before the food arrived, needing to be somewhat presentable.

Throwing on a pair of sleeping shorts and tank top, I

went to pour myself a glass of wine, while I waited for the delivery guy to arrive. Once he'd dropped off the food, I set the table and hurried to Cole's room to tell him dinner was ready.

Pushing his door open, I leaned my head in and whispered, "Dinner's here. I got your favorite, Italian." When he didn't answer, I walked further into the room, I saw that he was passed out, exhaustion had taken over and it looked like he was done for the evening. Sitting down next to him in his huge bed, I ran a hand over his hair and kissed his forehead. "Goodnight, babe, I love you." Leaving him to rest, I closed the door behind me and sent a quick text to Addison.

COME OVER, COLE'S PASSED OUT AND I HAVE ITALIAN.

Chapter Twenty-Five

OPEN UP, I'M HERE!

Smiling at my text from Addison, I jumped up off of the couch and ran to the door, pulling it open as quickly as I could. Being in the hospital every day with Cole, and Addison not being able to come visit due to her pregnancy, had left me feeling deprived of my best friend. I squealed as I rubbed her belly hoping for a baby bump, but knowing full well there wouldn't be one, yet.

Following my hands she grabbed her belly and laughed loudly. "Well hello to you too. I guess I need to get used to this, people paying attention to the baby and not me, that is." She pouted her lip out jokingly.

I smiled as I pulled her into a tight hug. "Gosh, I've missed you. I feel like I haven't seen you in forever, I know it hasn't really been that long, but shit, being cooped up in that hospital gave me a serious case of cabin fever." We both laughed and she followed me into the kitchen. "Want anything to eat? I have plenty, Cole's out for the night, so his will go to waste if you don't eat it." Reaching across the bar

Addison grabbed my plate, of course, she always wanted whatever was on my plate. "Hey, that's mine" I teased.

Pretending to sneeze on it, she laughed. "Mine now, besides you can't deny a pregnant person food, especially when it looks this delicious." Laughing, I conceded, knowing she was correct and also knowing that what Cole had on his plate was just as good.

After we devoured our dinner, me out of sheer starvation from earlier events and Addison out of pure pregnancy hunger, we sat on the couch in the living room and caught up on everything I'd been missing since Cole had been admitted into the hospital. Addison was going over her outfit for the annual Cartwright Christmas party this weekend. "I've narrowed it down to two dresses, one is red and one is silver. I bought both of them pre pregnancy, but I should be able to fit into them still. What are you wearing?" she asked.

Shit, what am I going to wear? I thought. "You know, I'm not really sure. First off, I have to make sure Cole is up for it, I can't take him if he's still not fully recuperated. As for an outfit, I'm thinking I'll have to go shopping and see what I can find."

We talked about all of the parties that were coming up for a bit and then Addison wanted to get more into the details of where Cole and I were going from here. "So, now that he is out of the hospital what are your plans? Are you going to stay here with him, or are you going to go home and just pick up where the two of you left off?"

I thought about my response before I said anything. "Well, to be perfectly honest, I hadn't really thought about it. I know I want to stay here and take care of him as long as he needs me, but I have my house and need to be there, too. Besides, it's not like he asked me to move in with him, we just got back together for goodness sakes. I'm sure we need some time to readjust now that he is home from the hospital."

"Well, I think you should move in with him, you know

he wants you to. Besides, you can rent your house, its prime real estate and you'd make a killing considering it's already paid for."

I laughed. "Actually, he hasn't said anything about it, so I can't just assume."

"Well, I'd love to have you here, if that's what you are wondering." A sleepy voice from behind us said. We both whipped around and stared at Cole standing there in nothing but a pair of boxers. *Damn, he looked sexy as hell.* I blushed, looking down as he walked closer towards the both of us. "I'm serious, I'd love for you to move in here with me."

Looking back up at him again I smiled. "Why don't we discuss this later?"

"Oh, I think now is perfect." Addison chimed in. I slapped her leg, getting up to walk over to Cole.

I wrapped my arms around his waist as I pushed up onto my tip toes, kissing his neck. "I have some bad news, I kind of ate your dinner. I didn't think you were going to wake up and I didn't want to waste it. Well, that and Addison ate my dinner, because she is a huge heifer." I said, turning back to her and sticking my tongue out teasingly.

"Are you trying to change the subject?" He whispered, grinning at me as he playfully kissed my lips.

"Kind of, why don't you throw me a bone, I wasn't really expecting this, we just got you out of the hospital. I think our first priority should be you fully recovering before we go making any major decisions."

Addison coughed, "chicken shit," behind me. Spinning around on my heels I glared at her, giving her my best shut your mouth look.

She smiled, lifting her shoulders and widening her eyes. Gosh, I loved her and she was my best friend, but sometimes she didn't know when to just shut up. "Addison, weren't you just leaving? I'm sure Case is ready for you to get home."

She laughed loudly, pretending to get up off the couch

like she was already nine months pregnant. "I suppose I'll go if you're kicking me and my unborn child out of your luxurious penthouse suite." I'm sure she could see the steam pouring out of my ears as I followed her to the door.

"Bye, Addison," Cole yelled from the living room, chuckling loud enough for the both of us to hear him.

"I'm so kicking your ass. You never know when to shut up!"

"Oh, get over it, you know you want to move in, you just don't have the balls to tell him." I stood there quietly for a minute, was she right; was I ready to move in with Cole or did I still need some time? Damn her for even putting me in the predicament of having to think about and potentially discuss my options.

Yanking me into a hug, Addison squeezed me tight. "Quit over thinking it, just go with the flow. You love him, he loves you. Case and I love you both, and we want to see you two happy, with everything you've both been through you deserve it."

I sighed heavily. "I'll think about it, but I'm not going to bring it up to him. If he wants me to move in with him then he's got to make it happen. I'm not going to force it. I have my house and I love it there, so I'm not in a rush."

She smiled, sauntering towards the elevator as she looked over her shoulder. "Don't worry, I'll make sure he brings it up." She laughed and jumped in the elevator, trying to escape the slew of expletives that she knew were about to fly out of my mouth. *Damn her.*

Walking back into the living room, I could see Cole sitting at the bar in the kitchen, "Babe, would you come in here for a minute," he called out to me.

I froze in my tracks; *please, don't bring up us moving in together*, I thought to myself as I forced my feet to move my body towards the kitchen. "What's up," I asked reaching for a bottle of water as I leaned against the counter.

"So you ate my dinner and after all of that sex we had earlier, I'm pretty starving."

I smiled as a plan popped into my head. "I did and it was absolutely delish, might I add, but if you can go without dinner I think I have a great dessert idea in mind." Opening the refrigerator door, I pulled out the can of whip cream and held it up, smiling at Cole.

He flew out of his seat and had my body pinned against the counter before I could even get the lid off of the can of whip cream. Laughing, he pulled the can from my hand, set it on the counter and had my shirt over my head, I couldn't even playfully resist. Grabbing the can he flipped it upside down and pressed the white dispenser, until cold whip cream covered my chest, right below my collar bone. Gripping my ass Cole picked me up and set me on top of the counter, so I was face to face with him and more assessable to his mouth. Tracing his tongue over the whip cream on my chest sent chills down my spine, he was sure to get all of it, before slowly bringing his lips back to mine so I could taste the sweetness on his mouth.

"Much better than dinner," he said as his lips pressed against mine. Without giving me time to agree, he had me leaned back and a trail of cream was being drawn from my breasts to my just below my belly button. Making his way down my body, he smiled up at me as he reached the bottom of the trail, a devilish grin spreading over his face as his hands began to tug at my shorts, "Now, for the real dessert."

Chapter Twenty-Six

"Wow, you look absolutely beautiful." Cole's arms wrapped around my waist as I looked over myself in the mirror, pleased with the outfit I'd found on my quick shopping trip the other night. I'd stumbled upon a sale at my favorite boutique and came across a long sleeved sparkly gold cocktail dress, it was just right for the Cartwright's annual Christmas party.

"Thank you." Turning in Cole's arms, I glanced over my shoulder to admired the way the dress dipped down to my lower back, exposing every inch of my bare back.

"You know, between the back of this dress and the length I feel like more skin is showing than covered." I smiled at his observation and planted a light kiss on his neck, inhaling my favorite smell of his cologne.

"I figured that'd be a good thing?" Leaning down I stepped into my matching six inch strappy stilettos, running a hand up the full length of my leg, teasing Cole on my way back up.

"You're fucking killing me, babe!" Cole exclaimed as he ran his hand through his tousled hair.

"Hello!" Teresa shouted when she opened the front door to Cole and me. It was the first time everyone had the chance to see Cole since he'd been released from the hospital. She pulled both of us into a hug, and then we were quickly being passed around the grand living room from person to person. Everyone in attendance was focused on hearing how Cole was doing since the accident.

After we'd been passed to the seventh group of guests, I saw Addison and Casey sitting in the living room. Releasing Cole's hand, I excused myself as he continued talking to his group of adoring fans. Grabbing a glass of champagne from a server I walked over to see my friends.

"Well, hello there preggers," I whispered to Addison, pulling her into a hug.

"Shhh! You know I haven't made the announcement, yet. Case won't let me until we're past the first trimester."

I smiled, pointing to her faux cocktail. "Hence, the fruit punch cosmo." We all laughed. Leaning in I hugged Casey. "Case, how have you been, making sure this one has everything her little heart desires?"

He smiled and kissed the top of my head. "Of course, we wouldn't want our favorite princess to want for anything, now would we?" Addison scrunched her nose and shot us both a mean glare.

After an hour or so of mingling, Cole finally made his way over to me, Addison and Casey. "Well, well, look who it is, the main event," Case joked with Cole.

Wrapping an arm around my waist, Cole pulled me closer to his side as he responded to Casey, "Main event in the flesh," he laughed as he shook Casey's hand. "Addison, you're looking lovely, how's that cocktail?" Cole asked, winking at her while we all laughed.

The party went on for hours before guests finally started making their way home. I could tell Cole was getting tired. "You ready to call it a night?" I asked, kissing his cheek.

He smiled down at me, "getting there, why don't we start making the rounds to tell everyone goodbye?"

Teresa and Theo were the last one's we needed to say goodbye to before leaving, other than Addison and Casey. "We are getting ready to head out; we had such a wonderful evening, as usual." I said, hugging the both of them together.

"You're leaving?" Teresa looked confused.

"Yes, it's been a long night for Cole, and we should probably get home." Teresa looked up at Theo, and then back to Cole and me. "Addison has obviously already had a case of pregnancy brain, she didn't tell you we were doing Christmas tomorrow morning?"

Each year on Christmas morning the Cartwright's and my family would get together and we'd all open gifts, have breakfast, and spend the day together. Addison and I would play with all of our new toys and we'd watch old home videos of past Christmas'. After my parent's passed, we continued the tradition and this year would be no different.

"Theo and I figured since you and Addison both have Cole and Casey you would want to spend the actual morning of Christmas together, so we decided we'd have our family Christmas tomorrow instead, is that okay?"

Looking to Cole, he nodded. "Well, it looks like we're in."

Teresa clapped and whispered to the both of us, "We'll get the rest of the guests on their merry way, so we can get ready for the pj swap."

Directing Cole into my bedroom at the Cartwright's, he collapsed onto my bed and looked at me puzzled. "Pj swap, should I be worried about this?"

Laughing, I lay down next to him and grabbed his hand. "It's a family tradition, well it was my family's tradition, but once my mom explained it to Teresa she adopted it, also. Each year on Christmas Eve, before I'd go to bed my parents would give me a new pair of pajamas, that way when my parents took pictures on Christmas morning and 'sent them back to

Santa' I wouldn't be dressed in old pj's, rather a pretty new picture worthy pair."

Cole chuckled, "Only you and Addison would worry about what your pajamas looked like on Christmas morning."

Sitting up, I planted a kiss on his lips. "You say it like it's a thing of the past, we're still worried what we look like in our pictures to Santa." I winked, getting up off of the bed, slowly pulling my dress over my shoulders. Cole's eyes watching intently as it slipped down my legs and I stood there in front of him in nothing but six inch stilettos and a pair of lace panties.

Walking back over to the bed, I climbed on top of his lap and leaned down towards his lips and whispered, "Fortunately for us, pajamas are optional at the current moment". One of his hands gripped my ass, as the other worked its way into my hair, pulling my lips right onto his. Reaching for his collar, I quickly began working my way down the buttons, until I could free him entirely. The dim moonlight shining into the room lit up the muscles on his chest and I admired them for a moment, soaking it all in before he flipped me onto my back and took my mouth again, this time grazing my lower lip with his teeth, as his hands made their way towards my panties.

"You sure this is okay, here?" It was cute that he was nervous to have sex in the Cartwright's house.

I didn't give myself time to think about it, I didn't care where we were I just wanted him. "Yes, it's fine" I exclaimed breathy.

Just as his hands began tugging at my panties the door flew open and Addison was standing there staring at the two of us. Cole jumped off of me and was standing at my bedside like a statue, looking from me to Addison and back to me. I quickly grabbed his shirt and pulled it over my shoulder, as I jumped up and scurried over to the door where Addison was standing. "What in the hell, can't you knock?"

She snickered, "Oh, you know if mom finds you two in here like this, you're in big trouble!" Leaning around me she peered at Cole. "You too, buddy. They don't even like me and Case getting frisky in their house, and we're married." I laughed as I looked back at a shocked Cole. Pushing Addison out of the door, I closed it just in time for her to yell, "Put your clothes back on, it's time for pajamas."

"Is it just me, or can we never catch a break? I think I've had to talk myself down more times since I've met you then I've had to do my entire life," he said, looking down at his pants.

Giggling, I pulled off his shirt, tossed it at him and ran into my closet to grab a pair of yoga pants and a sweater. When I came out of the closet Cole was buttoning his shirt. Taking his hands off of his shirt I began buttoning the remaining buttons and when I finished I kissed his lips lightly. "I'm sorry she interrupted, I promise I'll make it up to you. Come on, let's go see what kind of pajamas we got this year." Grabbing his hand I pulled him down the stairs and into the living room where Teresa, Theo, Casey, and Addison were all sitting with hot chocolate, waiting on the two of us with newly wrapped pajamas in hand.

The very next morning came way too quickly, as my cell phone chimed at 6:15 A.M.

GET UP, SANTA CAME LAST NIGHT! ;)

Grunting at my phone, I shook Cole. "Babe, wake up, Santa came last night." Laughing at what I'd just said, I shoved my phone in his face, so he could see the text Addison had just sent. He grunted as he drug himself out of bed, taking me along with him.

Teresa had a wonderful spread prepared for breakfast. We all ate, until we could consume no more, and then it was time to open presents. Like two little giddy children, Addison and I ran into the living room and plopped ourselves down directly in front of the Christmas tree, waiting on the rest of the clan to follow us in.

Casey looked at Cole laughing. "Do you see what we have to look forward to with these two? They're worse than children."

Teresa finagled her way through them and took a picture of the two of us sitting in front of the tree in our brand new pajamas, like she had done every year for as long as I could remember. "Alright girls, make sure everyone has a gift before you go tearing through all of them." Teresa knew if she didn't remind us, we'd have everything ripped open in a matter of minutes.

Sitting between Cole's legs in piles of wrapping paper and presents, I leaned back onto his chest and looked over at Case and Addison, and then Teresa and Theo, taking in all of my family. "This has been the best Christmas I have had in years. I love y'all so much."

Everyone smiled in agreement as Theo stood and walked towards the television, flipping it on before saying, "Now for another tradition, it wouldn't be Christmas without some old home videos." He pressed play on the DVD player and before we knew it a young Addison and Reagan were dancing and singing Christmas songs in front of the giant tree.

I relaxed further into Cole's chest and watched as childhood memories came flooding back. The tears beginning to flow as I heard my parent's voices in the background and before I knew it my mom and Teresa had joined the two of us on screen and we were all four singing and dancing. My mom was twirling me around in her arms before my dad came and joined in. *Gosh, I missed them so much.*

Kissing my head, Cole whispered into my ear, "You okay?" I nodded and his arms wrapped around me. "I love you, babe."

Smiling behind tear filled eyes, I squeezed his leg. "That's my mom and dad."

He sighed into my hair, squeezing me tighter. "Thank you for sharing this with me," he whispered quietly enough for only me to hear, before turning my face to kiss away the falling tears.

Chapter Twenty-Seven

After spending an early Christmas with the Cartwright's we continued rolling right into a slew of other holiday parties. It seemed like we were getting ready each and every night for something different, from client cocktail holiday parties to grand fundraising events where we were bidding on items to raise money to ensure the children's pediatric center had enough gifts for all of the kids in the hospital. Christmas with Cole had been unbelievable.

His living room was transformed into a winter wonderland. I'd gone to work early one morning and when I'd gotten back that night the entire living room was covered in green garland that had beautiful hand painted ornaments attached to it, bright red poinsettias lined the rooms and fireplace, and the fresh scent of pine took over my nose as I took in the giant Christmas tree that had been perfectly decorated. I'd stopped dead in my tracks when I saw what was sitting next to the Christmas tree. Walking over to the gold box, I picked it up and ran my fingers over the top of it, a tear rolling down my cheek as I did. Footsteps behind me pulled me out of the flood of memories that had instantly come over me.

"I hope you don't mind?" Cole asked, and I turned around to stare up into those beautiful eyes of his. I couldn't express my feelings in words, so I just kissed him instead. I kissed him long and hard, ensuring he knew exactly how thankful I was for him in that very moment.

After catching his breath, he smiled down at me, wrapping his arms around my waist. "I know how important the holidays were to you and your family, so after seeing those movies I talked to Teresa and Theo and asked if they had anything that would bring back those great memories from your past, turns out they had a few things." I smiled wondering what else I was going to get.

"Now, before you ask for everything at once I want you to know, I have a plan for when and where I'm going to give you each of the things they have given to me, so don't ruin the surprise. It's not going to be a long drawn out process, it just won't all come at once. Firsts things first, Teresa gave me the angel tree topper that your parents bought the year you were born and I thought that it would be perfect for the top of our tree, so wait right here, let me grab the step stool and I'll be right back."

Opening the gold box, I gently pulled the porcelain angel out, holding her delicately in my hands. She was just as I remembered her the very last time I'd put her on the tree with my parents. Her body draped in a beautiful white gown, sparkling silver angel wings that flanked her back, and a gold halo resting atop of her dark brown hair, she was beautiful. My parents bought her the year I was born and each year when my dad would pick me up to place her on the tip top of the tree, my parents would tell me that they were so lucky to have a daughter who was just as beautiful as Heaven's angels.

Cole rushed back in with the step stool, placing it as close to the tree as he could get it. Then reaching for my hand, helping me climb to the top of the stool. I still had to stand on

157

my tiptoes to reach the top. I gently placed my angel on the top of the Christmas tree, just as Cole snapped a picture with his phone.

"What do you think?" I asked.

Helping me down and taking me into his arms he whispered, "She's beautiful, just like you."

I squeezed his hips, pulling him as close as I could get him. "Thank you, Cole, this really means the world to me. I miss them so much, but I love sharing them with you." Kissing my forehead, we stood there for a few minutes before I broke the silence, "So, what do I get next?" I asked, laughing into his chest.

"I knew I shouldn't have told you about the rest of them."

It'd been a few days since Cole started the gift giving and I was getting anxious, trying to figure out what I'd get next. Christmas morning I was pleasantly surprised when I'd opened the next gift, a picture of me, Mom, and Dad the year we spent Christmas in Colorado. We were outside next to the snowman Addison and I built together. I was eight years old, and that had been one of the best Christmas's I'd ever had. "Did Teresa tell you about this Christmas when she gave you the picture?"

He smiled gently. "She explained everything as minimally as possible; I think she wanted you to be able to share the actual stories with me instead of her."

Leaning back against the couch I closed my eyes, and I began to see snow fall, it was like I was right back in Colorado. "Addison and I begged our parents to take us to see snow for Christmas, one of the kids in our class convinced us that if it didn't snow Santa wouldn't bring us gifts. I remember mom and Teresa didn't want to go, they already had both houses decorated, the gifts were all wrapped and the annual Christmas party was planned for the day before Christmas Eve. Addison decided if we could talk our dad's into it, then our mom's would eventually cave, so we did.

"The afternoon of the Christmas party we cornered our Dad's while they were running around making sure everything was ready. We'd decided I would plead the case, after all, I'd known from a very young age I was going to be an attorney. So I went for it, Addison chiming in as needed, and before we knew it, the night before Christmas Eve my dad was calling his assistant to have her arrange our flights and book us a log cabin at a ski resort in the mountains of Colorado."

Opening my eyes I looked at him and a grin grew across his face. "So even at eight years old you had the men in your life eating out of the palm of your hand?"

Laughing, I shook my head. "I wouldn't say that, there were times I didn't get what I wanted, granted they were few and far between, but nonetheless, they occurred." His facial expression spoke for the words that were running through his head, and I laughed harder. "We were spoiled, I know, but trust me, we were thankful, still are. There isn't a day that goes by that we don't know how blessed we are."

Handing him a gift, we rolled into the other presents that were under the tree. We'd spent the next few hours opening presents, after we were finished we laid down on the floor in front of the fireplace and looked at all of the wrapping paper spread throughout the room. "I think we may have gone a bit overboard on gifts, what do you think?"

Cole pulled me closer to him, so my head was resting against his chest. "Just imagine when we have kids." My heart skipped, and then it was instantly slamming into my chest as I tried to replay the words that had just come out of his mouth. I could feel his body shaking under me as he squeezed me tight. "I thought we'd put a stop to those panic attacks?" he asked, as I tried to calm my nerves, his body still shaking with laughter. *We did, until you decided to bring up kids, you must have really hit your head in that fall.* I thought to myself. Rubbing the length of my arm, Cole spoke in between laughs, "Babe, I can feel your heart pounding against my ribcage, calm down, you aren't going to get pregnant by lying next to me. I'm just talking about the future, one day down the road." Sucking in a long breath I tried my best to calm myself down.

Lying there for a few minutes in silence I was able to calm my nerves, just in time for the doorbell to ring. Cole sat up and looked at me. "Are you expecting company?"

I shook my head. "No, are you?" He shook his head no, as he stood up and walked towards the door. Jumping up, I started grabbing the wrapping paper that was spread throughout the living room, trying to clean up for whomever had decided to drop in. Before I could get it all together I heard the one voice on this earth I could pick out a million miles away.

Looking towards the entryway of the living room I saw Addison scurrying in as Case followed behind her, gifts stacked so high in his arms he couldn't even see over them. Laughing, I ran towards her, "Merry Christmas!" I shouted, hugging her so tight.

Casey passing me as he tried to find a place to put all of the gifts, "Merry Christmas, Case."

He laughed. "Right back atcha, babe," as the gifts came toppling out of his hands and crashing to the floor.

Laughter erupted amongst all of us and Addison was quickly at his side, pulling him down to the floor to sit. "It's okay, babe, we were going to end up down here anyway." And on that note Cole and I cozied up next to the tree and the four of us began our first annual Christmas morning tradition.

Chapter Twenty-Eight

"Babe, come on, we are going to miss our flight." Cole shouted from the front door.

I was trying my best to move as fast as I could, pulling my carry on behind me as I ran out of his bedroom. "I'm sorry, it's just a little hard to get everything together when you have absolutely no idea where you are going." Planting a kiss on his lips, I hurried out the door towards the elevator. Pressing the button as many times as I could, in the hopes of making it arrive faster.

"You know pushing the button a thousand times doesn't increase your chances of it getting here any quicker, right?" Scrunching my nose, I shot him a funny face as the bell chimed and the doors slid open.

The stewardess handed Cole a Yuengling and me a glass of wine as the plane flew west over the Gulf of Mexico. "Ma'am, would you mind telling me where we're headed?" She looked at Cole, who shot her an evil glare, and she quickly apologized and scurried off. "Seriously, even the flight attendants know it's a surprise?"

He chuckled. "Yes, now quit trying to ruin it. We'll be

there before you know it. Once we land, you'll put two and two together and then it'll no longer be a surprise, so just appease me for a few more hours, please."

"Fine" I said, pretending to pout as I looked out the window and sipped my wine.

Three hours later the jolt of the tires hitting the ground woke me out of my nap and I looked at Cole, who was squirming in his seat like a child. Looking out the window all I could see was white snow and mountains for miles. "Umm, Cole, I don't think I have enough clothes to keep me warm in this weather."

Smiling, he pointed to the coat rack on board and said, "Don't worry, I've got you covered." Being that we were seated in first class we were able to get off the plane quickly. After getting our luggage, we walked towards the exit of the airport where our rental SUV was waiting for us, before going outside Cole helped me into my coat. "You ready, it's pretty freezing out there?" Smiling, I reached for his hand and we exited out into the frigid weather.

Opening the passenger's door I jumped in the car and turned on the heat as high as I could get it. Cole threw the luggage in the back and jumped in the front seat and then drove off. Now, I was the one squirming in my seat like a child. "Okay, can you please tell me where we are going?"

He glanced over at me and smiled. "If you haven't figured it out, yet, then I'm not going to ruin it."

"I hate surprises, are we going skiing?" I asked, hoping he would possibly indulge me in a round of twenty questions.

"Yes." He smiled, watching the road as the snow came down around us.

"How long is it going to take us to drive there?"

He looked down at the clock and back to the road. "Probably twenty minutes, no more questions, please."

I leaned over and kissed his cheek. "Fine, I'm just so excited."

Turning off of the main highway, we started heading up the side of a huge mountain. The sun was beginning to set in the distance as we made our way further and further up the mountain.

When we got to the top Cole looked over at me and smiled. "You ready?"

I began bouncing in my seat, "yes, the suspense is killing me!" I shouted.

Turning off of the road he began driving slowly down a long drive. By the looks of it the snow plow had just recently come through, the mounds of snow pushed off of the driveway were stacked to my shoulders and before I looked back ahead of me the car came to a complete stop. Opening the door I jumped out of the SUV as my jaw instantly hit the ground below me. I looked to Cole who had emerged from the SUV and then back to the quaint log cabin sitting before me.

I ran towards Cole as fast as I could, tackling him into a pile of snow as I grabbed the sides of his face and took his mouth, my tongue shoving past his lips while my hands grasped at his hair. His arms wrapping around me as I devoured his mouth, pulling away from his lips his hands flew to my hips as I straddled his lap in a pile of snow.

"You have no idea how amazing you are. I cannot believe you booked the exact cabin we came to when I was eight." Grinning up at me with those gorgeous golden eyes, he just laid there, relishing in the moment. Kissing him quickly, I jumped off of his lap and pulled him up, as I tugged his hand towards the cabin. "Come on, I have to show you around. You're going to love it here."

When we got to the porch Cole pulled the keys out, but before he opened the door he pulled me into his arms and kissed me. "I wish I could have brought you here for Christmas, but I figured New Years was second best."

Pressing my lips onto his, I grabbed the keys from his hands. "This is perfect, Cole."

The lock clicked with the turn of the key and I opened the door and stepped in flipping on the light switch to my right. I looked around the open log cabin and memories of being there almost twenty years ago came flooding back. My smile grew even bigger as I felt Cole's hands wrap around me. Not only had I made amazing memories here with my family, but now I was going to be making memories with Cole, as well. Cole slipped my coat off and hung it on the rack next to the door.

I pointed to the corner of the living room and said, "That's where the tree was. It was so small and there were no lights on it, all we had were paper ornaments that Addison and I made and hung on it with some fishing line we found in a drawer. We got in midday on Christmas Eve and everything was already closed, so Addison, Dad, Theo, and I went out in search of a tree we could cut down. When we found it I remember thinking it was perfect, it was no taller than the two of us girls. We helped chop it down and Dad and Theo set it up right there."

Pulling him into the dining room, I ran my fingers over the wood table. It was the same one that had been there before, dark black wood with eight huge matching chairs surrounding it. "Every Christmas we would get a new board game, and that year Addison and I begged for Mall Madness. The credit card machine was new and improved from the original and we were dying to get our hands on it. Mom and Teresa spent hours in the kitchen preparing dinner while Dad and Theo suffered through three hours of Addison and I giggling and making fun of them buying all of the girly clothes."

I took Cole through every room of the cabin and told him story after story, remembering something different in each room. By the time I'd given him the entire tour, I was sure he had relived every moment I'd spent in the cabin that Christmas.

After getting all of our bags into the house, we decided we'd call it a night and get to bed, so we'd be ready for our morning on the slopes tomorrow. Falling into bed I was knocked out in a matter of minutes, especially once Cole started rubbing my back. That night I dreamt of my parents meeting Cole and what it would have been like. *Of course Mom loved him, Dad on the other hand was a bit harder to win over, but after spending the day with us and seeing how much he really loved me Dad was on board.* At the sun peeking through the cabin window I stretched and looked over at a sleeping Cole, smiling at the memory of last night's dream. "Babe, wake up." I shook his body and he jumped at the touch of my cold hands. Laughing, I apologized and I climbed out of bed and hopped into the hot shower.

Cole was all suited up in his ski gear when I closed the back door behind me, the slopes were right beyond the back yard, so we didn't have far to go. He helped me into all of my gear, and before I knew it we were pulling our goggles down as we headed for the slopes. "You know I'm pretty good, right?" I joked with Cole as he looked me up and down.

"Oh, you may be good, but I guarantee you won't beat me." Laughing, I took off down the mountain, listening to him yell after me. We spent the entire day racing down all different kinds of slopes, some I'd win and some Cole would win. Although, I let him have all of the ones he won. It was a perfect day and by the time we got back to the cabin we were exhausted. We'd showered, shared a cup of hot chocolate and fell asleep on the couch in front of the blazing fire.

Chapter Twenty-Nine

"Do you have the champagne?" I yelled to Cole from in front of the television. We were two minutes away from midnight and the ball in Time Square was flashing as it was getting ready to begin its descent. He ran into the living room looking dashing as he insisted we dress up even though we weren't leaving the house. He had a bottle of champagne and two flutes in tow just in time for us to start the countdown together.

Standing there dressed to the nines, Cole in a sleek black Armani tuxedo with a gold tie that matched his beautiful eyes and me in a black lace dress that had a slit from the bottom straight up the top of my thigh. Cole quickly filled our champagne flutes and we both yelled with the crowd on TV, "10, 9, 8, 7, 6, 5, 4, 3, 2, 1...HAPPY NEW YEAR!" We screamed, as Cole slid his arms around my waist, pulling me in for a New Year's kiss that had me seeing fireworks of my own.

Releasing me he whispered, "Happy New Year, baby" and lifted his champagne flute to toast with me. We clinked glasses and both lifted our flutes to our mouths. Turning to reach for the bottle that was sitting on the table behind us I filled my glass. I was turning back around to ask Cole if he'd like anymore and I gasped when I saw him down on one knee. I slowly set my champagne flute down, so I wouldn't drop it and my hands flew straight to my face, covering my mouth that was hanging wide open. Reaching into his pocket he pulled out a black velvet box.

"Reagan Larson, I love you, everything about you, the way you giggle when something is funny, your earth shattering smile, the way your cheeks flush when you're embarrassed, your passion for the things you care most about, your dedication, I even love your panic attacks, but mostly I love who I am when I'm with you. I can't imagine feeling this way with any other person, Reagan. You are my world, my life, and without you I have nothing. There is nothing on this earth I'd rather have than your hand in marriage and to build a future with you."

Opening the velvet box, I choked back tears thinking it couldn't be true, sitting in the slit of the black box was my mother's three carat cushion cut halo engagement ring that my father had proposed to her with. The tears that pricked my eyes began to flood down my cheeks, and Cole reached for my hand. "Reagan Larson, would you do me the greatest honor of becoming my wife?" Shaking my head yes over and over again, he slid the ring onto my finger as he stood and worked his hands up my waist, cupping my face and kissing my lips for the first time as my *fiancé*.

Looking into my eyes he smiled as he whispered, "Is that a yes? I know you shook your head, but you never said it?"

I laughed through the tears, "Yes, Cole Conrad, there is no other person I'd rather spend the rest of my life with than you."

The End... For Now

UPCOMING BOOKS
Fighting For Her
(Cole Conrad's Point of View – Releasing in 2014)

About the Author

K.S. Smith is a twenty seven year old aspiring new contemporary romance author. When she is not writing you will most likely find her nose in a book, spending time with her family and friends or dedicating her time to the military through her favorite non-profit organization.

K.S. Smith was born and raised in Tampa, FL and continues to build her life there in her new home with her boyfriend of ten years who will hopefully one day put all book boyfriends to shame with an out of this world proposal.

https://www.facebook.com/kssmith23
https://twitter.com/kssmith_23
https://www.goodreads.com/author/show/7215509.K_S_Smith

5915273R00103

Made in the USA
San Bernardino, CA
24 November 2013